LONG TIME COMING

HOT RODS

JAYNE RYLON

Email: contact@jaynerylon.com
Website: www.jaynerylon.com

Sign Up for the Naughty News!
Twenty-five subscribers win prizes in each edition!
www.jaynerylon.com/newsletter

Social Media:
Facebook: Facebook.com/jaynerylon
Twitter: @JayneRylon

Shop for autographed books, apparel, goodies and more at:
www.jaynerylon.com/shop

OTHER BOOKS BY JAYNE RYLON

Available Now

COMPASS BROTHERS
Northern Exposure
Southern Comfort
Eastern Ambitions
Western Ties

COMPASS GIRLS
Winter's Thaw
Hope Springs
Summer Fling
Falling Softly

HOT RODS
King Cobra
Mustang Sally
Super Nova
Rebel On The Run
Swinger Style
Barracuda's Heart
Touch of Amber
Long Time Coming

MEN IN BLUE
Night is Darkest
Razor's Edge
Mistress's Master
Spread Your Wings
Wounded Hearts

PARANORMAL DOUBLE PACK
Picture Perfect
Phoenix Incantation
Paranormal Double Pack Boxset

PICK YOUR PLEASURES
Pick Your Pleasure
Pick Your Pleasure 2

PLAY DOCTOR
Dream Machine
Healing Touch

POWERTOOLS
Kate's Crew
Morgan's Surprise
Kayla's Gift
Devon's Pair
Nailed To The Wall
Hammer It Home

RACING FOR LOVE
Driven
Shifting Gears
Racing For Love Boxset

RED LIGHT (STAR)
Through My Window
Star
Can't Buy Love
Free For All
Red Light Boxset

SINGLE TITLES
Nice and Naughty
Report For Booty
Where There's Smoke

AUDIOBOOKS
Barracuda's Heart
Devon's Pair
Dream Machine
Hammer it Home
Kate's Crew
Kayla's Gift
King Cobra
Long Time Coming
Morgan's Surprise
Mustang Sally
Nailed to the Wall
Nice and Naughty
Night is Darkest
Powertools
Rebel on the Run
Report For Booty
Super Nova
Swinger Style
Touch of Amber

———

Coming Soon

MEN IN BLUE
Bound For You

PICK YOUR PLEASURES
Pick Your Pleasure 3

PLAY DOCTOR
Developing Desire

SINGLE TITLE
4-ever Theirs

LONG TIME COMING
HOT RODS, BOOK 8

Some things are worth the wait.

Tom London has done a pretty damn good job. Despite an illness that stole his young wife years ago, he's raised his biological son, and several adopted ones, to be fine men. The Hot Rods might be unconventional, but they're hardworking, hard-playing, and hard-loving. Tom couldn't ask for anything more—except perhaps an equally fierce love of his own. And he's got his eye on a luscious candidate. Ms. Wilhelmina Brown, a longtime widow with more than enough sass in her step to take him on.

Willie has a lot in common with Tom. She's raised two wonderful daughters, both now married into the Hot Rods family, and lived through her own tragedy, having lost her husband in a horrific accident. More than two decades later, she and Tom still live with the ghosts of their pasts, but she'd have to be dead herself not to feel the man's effect on her libido. They already share a mutual respect; perhaps they can each be what the other needs in more tangible ways...

As Tom and Willie take one step closer, an explosive revelation shoots them several steps back. But that bombshell turns out to be just a precursor to something potentially worse...potentially deadly...and potentially enough to keep the mature lovers apart forever.

DEDICATION

For Kelli Collins. It might have taken forty-one books, but here we are. Together at last!

Another huge thank you to my beta readers: Fedora, Casey, Jenna, Shari and Brandi.

PROLOGUE

Wilhelmina Brown couldn't believe she'd been married for seven full years. People had said she and Steven would never last when they'd tied the knot the day after high school graduation. She was happy to prove them wrong. Looking at the two precious children they'd made, who slept together on a pullout couch in the tiny yet spotless living room, she couldn't have been prouder or more content.

Hopefully, her husband would enjoy the dinner she'd cooked to celebrate their milestone and the time they'd had together. The roast was the prime cut of the latest slaughter from the Berry Family Farm down the road from the house they shared on the outskirts of town. She'd bartered some extra sewing to supplement her grocery money for the splurge. Rural Mississippi life had to have some perks. After all, inclusion certainly wasn't one of them.

She tried not to think of some people's outdated ignorance and the hatred they tried to inject into her relationship with Steven, simply because her skin was drastically darker than his. Or how he'd been passed over for promotions after he'd brought her to the company picnic. Or her guilt about the way even some lifelong friends had treated him, turned on him, since he dared to love her.

Not tonight.

Sometimes it felt as if it was them against the world. She was okay with that. With a partner like him at her back, she could manage pretty much anything.

Willie tidied the already neat kitchen then fussed with her hair and the skirt of the pink dress she'd made while she waited for her husband, who frequently doubled up on his shifts for overtime. Maybe they'd get lucky and the girls would sleep straight through the night. They were almost always in bed by the time their daddy got home. In the cramped quarters, they often woke up to sneak in a visit before Willie and Steven were ready to go to sleep in the house's single bedroom. She probably shouldn't let them stay up so late so often, but when she saw how happy the playtime made her children and her husband alike, she didn't have the heart to put her foot down.

Willie checked the clock on the wall.

Wouldn't it figure that Steven was running even later than usual?

She peeked in at the supper, breathed deep, drew the savory aroma into her lungs, then crumpled the tinfoil over the baking pan tighter to keep the meat warm without drying it out.

An hour later, it was pretty clear something had gone horribly wrong.

Willie sat with the phone on the kitchen table in front of her, twisting the spiral cord in her fingers as she waited for Steven to call and explain whatever fluke had kept him at the factory where he welded hot water heater tanks, or how he'd run out of gas, or...*something*.

He never did.

Instead, a loud triple knock on the front door had her shooting out of the kitchen chair so fast it toppled to the outdated harvest-gold linoleum behind her. The kids woke at the crash. Nola began to cry when Willie darted past her and her older sister—Amber, who comforted her sibling—to answer the door.

"Shush, it's okay," she lied to them as she paused, her fingers wrapped around the knob, afraid to turn it and change her life forever. Alternating red and blue washes of light painted her babies' lovely mocha skin ghastly unnatural shades.

Right then, she knew she'd relive this moment in her nightmares for the rest of her life.

The pounding on the door came again, startling her into action.

Before she could stop herself, she opened it—just a little, like Steven had shown her. She peeked from inside the safe haven they'd built together at the police officers standing on her cracked front stoop.

"Mrs. Brown?" the taller of the two asked with a grimace.

"Yes." Her heart pounded so fast and so hard that she had

trouble hearing her own voice. Or maybe it was merely a wisp compared to usual.

"I regret to inform you that there's been an accident." He paused and swallowed. "A bad one. It's your husband, ma'am."

"No!" As if it would block out the terrible news she'd never be able to unhear, she lifted the hem of her apron, covering her face with the gingham material Steven had salvaged from a stained tablecloth at the Salvation Army for her last birthday.

It seemed as if her children understood the cops when their wails escalated to shrieks. Or maybe that was her making those strangled sobs.

"He's hurt?" She tried to keep herself together in case she could go to him, help him to fight.

The stockier officer came to his partner's aid. "There was no chance for survival. The car was completely destroyed in the collision with a delivery truck. Then it spun off the road, crashed through the railing on Jefferson's Bridge and went into the river. With all the rain we've had lately, he washed away before anyone could even think of assisting. I'm very sorry."

Willie's knees buckled. She fell to the ground, gasping for air through the searing pain in her chest, which resulted from her shattering heart. Was this what Steven had felt like in those final moments?

If it weren't for the girls behind her, she would have let herself wither away and rejoin her husband. Amber and Nola screamed a chorus of "Momma, Momma!" endlessly, as if they could tell how desperately Willie needed a reason to pick herself up.

Somehow she would do it.

She had to.

For them, the only remaining pieces of her husband in the world.

⫷ONE

Twenty-One Years Later

"No!" Willie thrashed as she surfaced from her nightmare, her heart thundering every bit as wildly now as it had years before. The piercing pain never lessened. Each time she rehashed the darkest moment of her life, it stabbed her.

Over and over.

So she focused on separating reality from the lingering replay of her past. Something trapped her, keeping her from injuring herself or anyone around her with her desperate flailing. A man.

Not the police, who'd restrained her from flying into the night to join her husband, carried away by those flood waters. She shook her head to clear the last of the vision from her mind. It wasn't easy. Not tonight or any other.

Unlike every other time, though, she wasn't alone.

Strong arms banded around her, keeping her still. It would

be easy to maim herself or the guy sleeping beside her—fully dressed in shorts and a Hot Rods T-shirt—if left to her own reenacted grief. Unbelievably fit, he sheltered her, keeping her safe.

So different from the man she'd lost all those years ago. She breathed deep of his comforting scent. Unmistakable, it smelled something like the air outside his house. A mix of fresh green things from the garden he loved with a tinge of gasoline from his service station.

A hint of a smile crossed her face as he brought her to a place filled with promise instead of desolation.

Iron-willed and kindhearted, Tom London was always there for her.

At least he had been before he'd seen this side of her. What would he think now?

"Tommy," she whimpered, her voice a harsh crackle that would have annoyed her if she was awake enough or brave enough to give a crap right then.

"Yeah, it's me. I'm here. I've got you." He sat them up, rocking her gently, stroked her hair, and rubbed her back with endless patience that she couldn't bring herself to reject. Only the fact that he too had suffered a similar devastation allowed her to accept his comfort. Sometimes he even let her return the favor when he was missing his wife, who had died of cancer more than a decade earlier. He understood Willie like no one had before.

Unashamed, she cuddled against his solid chest. The wedding ring he wore on a chain around his neck came between them. They may have been sharing a bed, but that was about as intimate as things had ever gotten between her and the handsome garage owner. They'd made out a few times, sure. *Almost* had sex.

Inevitably, something had kept them apart.

Less than a month ago her daughter, Nola, and Tom's adopted son, Kaige, had made them grandparents. Willie couldn't believe her baby had a precious little one of her own and had gladly volunteered to help out during the tough adjustment period that came along with a new family. The kids lived across the driveway from Tom's house, above the garage Kaige worked at along with the rest of his misfit mechanic gang, Hot Rods.

Due to the complex polyamorous relationship among the group, Willie felt more comfortable…less intrusive…staying at Tom's house. With Quinn, another refugee from a devastating childhood—fifteen-year-old brother to one of the guys in Tom's collection of strays—taking up residence in the spare bedroom, there weren't a lot of options in the cozy cottage.

Tom had refused to let her sleep on the couch and she had insisted she wouldn't displace him. Though he was sexy as sin, he wasn't as young as their kids and squishy cushions could wrap a person's spine into a pretzel if he wasn't careful. Hence, her spot in the only available space…the other half of Mr. London's bed.

Same mattress, separate sides.

PJs all the time.

Him on top of the sheets while she dozed under them.

It could have been an awkward arrangement. Nothing she did with Tom was anything but natural, though. They were seasoned adults, her forty-six and him a few weeks short of fifty. So they pretended it was no big deal, even if they both seemed to take an awfully long time to fall asleep in each other's presence.

Tonight she was glad for his company. His friendship.

In the past year, since their kids had met, he'd become someone she confided in—relied on—during emotional times. That alone was enough to terrify her. Solo was her style.

It was safer that way.

Except Tom had a funny habit of sneaking beneath her guard, making her open up in ways she'd never dreamed possible for her again.

"Do you have nightmares a lot?" he wondered.

See, like this. She should brush him off and keep him from getting further entangled in her dysfunction. No matter how many times she cleared her throat, hating the raw sting her shouts had left behind, she couldn't seem to stop herself from admitting, "Some."

Another reason she'd avoided sleepovers with the mature yet ultra-desirable man.

When she would have pulled away, straightened her nightgown, then rolled over, pretending to sleep as she watched the glowing red numbers on the clock beside the bed countdown to dawn, he kept her close.

"Not so fast, Willie," he practically growled. "Why do I get the feeling *some* actually means *a lot*?"

"Because it does. Now leave me be so I can get some rest," she grumbled, though part of her secretly sighed, finally able to divulge her weakness to someone who might not judge her.

"Don't act like you're going to doze right off again. I never can when I dream of Michelle." His voice changed when he whispered his wife's name into the darkness.

Full of pain, even now.

"Did you know I met her once?" Willie felt as though she'd been keeping secrets, not admitting it before.

"You did?" He put a sliver of distance between them, only moving far enough to meet her stare. Despite the dim interior of the room, his sky-blue eyes glowed like lasers. "I bet she liked you very much. She didn't take shit from anyone either, though she had this awesome way of putting people in their place without letting them realize precisely what she was doing."

"Bless their hearts." Willie allowed Mississippi to roll thick off her tongue.

"Exactly." He laughed gruffly. At least for a few seconds, before he grew serious again. "It was at her shelter, wasn't it? Nola told me once that you'd used the services there when times were rough."

Thank God for her dark skin and the night, both of which should hide her flaming cheeks. Would she ever forgive herself for being such a failure? Probably not.

"Yes. I knew it was really a place for children who needed assistance. So I took the girls. She saw me huddled outside and invited me in. Told me she could tell how tired I was. Gave us food, clean clothes, and a place to freshen up since we were living in that stinky old van." Willie couldn't help it, a tear slipped down her cheek. She would have dashed it from her face, but Tom noticed and kissed it away. "Michelle was beautiful. Glowing with kindness. It was hard not to smile when I was around her. She had herself so together. I admired her."

"We all have good and bad days. I loved her through to the bottom of my soul, you know I did. But even she wasn't perfect. She left her dirty clothes on the floor and never put the cap back on the toothpaste, dumb shit like that. I remember arguing about stuff that didn't matter worth a damn…" He trailed off.

"Yeah, but the important things…she had those right." Willie shivered. "As we were about to leave the shelter, she took me aside, looked me straight in the eyes, and told me—"

Tom didn't press her to finish. Instead he kept up that maddening rock, lulling her into complacency. Suddenly, it poured out.

"She promised me that I wasn't a bad mom. That I was doing the best I could under the circumstances. And she gave me her card. Said that she would look into resources for adults, instead of children only, and that we should come back. Let her help us."

"You didn't take her up on it?" He groaned. "Why, Willie? We would have done whatever we could have."

She didn't doubt it. After all, that's how he'd ended up with not only his son Eli, but also custody of the other seven kids who'd grown up as Hot Rods.

"I tried, actually. A couple months went by before I could work up the nerve. I'd taken on some more seamstress jobs and had enough to do okay, relatively. Until the winter kept dragging on. Amber had a cough she couldn't shake from sleeping in the freezing car. I was worried about the girls. So I thought about what Michelle had said and I swallowed my embarrassment to go ask for help." She shook now in his hold. "When I went back, they told me she was unavailable to see us. At first, I thought she hadn't found anything and didn't want me bugging her about it. I understood. A few months later, they had that article about her that took up the whole front page of the newspaper."

"When she died." Tom sniffled now, too. "There's a copy in that box over on the dresser."

"I'm sorry." She hadn't meant to hurt him with her reminiscences.

"It's okay." He took a few deep breaths then said, "It's just that I know she would have hated letting you down. Even if it was because she was terminally ill. It happened so damn fast. We didn't have a lot of plans in place. For us personally and definitely not for the charity. The shelter had always been her baby and the garage mine, so I didn't know how to step in and I was too grief-stricken to hire the right people at first. We were young. Never expected something like that to happen. Things slipped through the cracks. *You* slipped through the cracks. Oh God, Willie. I'm sorry."

"Hang on, that's not why I told you that." She never wanted to wound him. "I only wanted to say that I understand. Why you still love her, I mean. She was special."

"I'm sure your Steven was, too." He hugged her harder. "I can't even imagine what it must have been like to get that news. Well, kind of. I remember the day I came home and found Michelle sitting at the kitchen table with a cup of tea. It was about a week after Valentine's Day and she was sitting there staring at the wilted roses I'd bought her. I looked at her and I knew. I just fucking knew. She didn't even last through the spring."

"Maybe that's why we're both so screwed up still?" Willie looked up to him, cupping his salt-and-pepper-stubbled cheek in her palm. "It was so unexpected. Over before you could really say goodbye."

"Worse for you." He shook his head. After a couple ragged breaths, he pushed on, as if refusing to lock everything away again now that they'd dragged it out into the open. "Will you tell me why you believe Steven's accident was your fault?"

The hiss that left her would have been appropriate if an arrow had punctured her lung and let the air wheeze out. Felt that way too. Direct hit.

For a moment the room spun.

"Hey, hey." Tom squeezed her tight. "I shouldn't have asked. If you're not ready—"

"No." In the dead of the night she found she wanted to share this with him once and for all. "It's okay. It's almost been a quarter of a century. If now's not the time, it never will be. And Tommy, I'm getting tired."

He knew she wasn't talking about her lack of sleep either.

"I know. Me too." He kissed her forehead.

For a moment, she wished he'd forget this talking nonsense and take action instead. It might be nice to blot out their sadness with bliss. She wouldn't know how to make a move on a man if her life depended on it though, having pretty much zero experience in modern dating, or dating at all for that matter, since she and Steven had been childhood sweethearts.

"We'd been getting harassing letters. Phone calls in the middle of the night. Threats spray-painted on the side of the house every once in a while. It wasn't really anything new, we'd been hearing that racial garbage since we were twelve and best friends." She paused. "But it seemed…different."

"How so?"

"More vicious. I got the feeling Steven wasn't even telling me everything. Like maybe there had been an incident at his job, too," she confessed. "I could tell he was hiding something. I should have pushed him to tell me. He could be overbearingly protective. Like some other man I know."

Tom shrugged as if it wasn't such a bad trait. "Can't say I blame him. I look out for my own."

"Yeah, well…" She took a shaky breath then closed her eyes as if it would shield her from what she was about to say. "I did a lot of poking around in the days after the *accident*. It was more of an on-purpose incident. There were too many things that didn't add up. The delivery truck driver said he saw another car tailing Steven, driving aggressively, shoving the car over the center line. You could see proof of it on the road. Skid marks from more than one car. The police said there was nothing they could do. The driver had been too busy trying to avoid Steven to get much more than a glimpse at the other vehicle. Old, dark paint, black or maybe blue. Not much to go on, you know?"

"Jesus." Tom clutched her to him.

"Who would do that to him?" It still ate at her. "He didn't have any enemies except those he'd made because of me. He was a nice man, a decent one, too. Like you said, it's okay to admit we're all flawed. Looking back, I think he wasn't so great at confrontation, or very motivated to improve. Passive, I guess you'd say. He never stood up to the people who bullied us, but what could he have done anyway?"

"It sounds like our styles were different. He shielded you by turning the other cheek and keeping you in the dark. Hell, that could have put you in more danger. What if they hadn't left you alone after they took care of him?"

"That's why I took the girls and left. We had nothing except what I could fit in a single suitcase when I ran, not that we had a heck of a lot more than that anyway. Nothing important. I hopped on the first bus headed north and went as far as the fare would take me."

"If I were him, I'd have opted for something more direct. I sure as shit would never have stood by and let a bunch of assholes threaten my family." Tom shook his head. "Sorry, Willie, I don't mean to speak ill of a dead man, but you know that's true."

She did. After all, in the past year alone she'd watched him wrestle custody of Quinn from his abusive mother, help Roman and Gavyn battle addiction issues, negotiate a deal to protect Kaelyn and Bryce from their Senator fathers, and heard stories about the lengths he'd gone to in order to make sure Sally could never be bothered by the religious cult she'd been born into. He was superhuman in her eyes.

A fixer.

A doer.

A lover.

Damn if that didn't make her burrow closer to him.

Tom cradled her, nuzzling her temple with his chin. "I think it's time we both admitted that we've spent so much time looking in the rearview mirror that we might have missed some of the scenery around us."

"That's true." Cutting him a break, she said, "You at least had reasons. You concentrated on helping others. The Hot Rods are thriving today because of you."

"Your daughters are pretty amazing women, too, Willie." He ran his fingers through her hair.

"Sometimes I think that's in spite of having me as their mom, not because of it." She shook her head.

"It's not. They're brave and hardworking, just like you. If your Steven were still here, he'd tell you that, too." Tom shifted, pulling her into his lap so he could look at her when he said,

"Actually, I think what our partners would say to us if they could, is that we should stop wishing for what's gone and make the most of what we have. Don't you think?"

It was impossible to argue when he stared into her eyes so intently.

So she nodded—a tiny shake of her head as she swallowed hard.

"Good." He smiled, slow and wide. "Then I think you should know I'm ready. To try this again. It's okay if you're not. I'm clearly not in a hurry. I *will* make you mine sooner or later, Ms. Brown."

The kids' name for her had her chuckling.

"You think that's funny?" He growled as he flipped them, holding himself above her on straight-locked arms. "I'm a patient man, but I'm not joking, Willie."

With him looming above her, it was impossible to argue how damn attractive he was. Parts of her she hadn't used in so long she thought they might have fallen off, stood up and cheered as he descended slowly, entrapping her in his heat and the cage made by his muscular frame.

It was one she wasn't sure she wanted to escape.

So when he let his head drop, his mouth lowering to within a hairsbreadth of her own, she didn't flinch from his touch or shy away from the raw emotion in his gaze.

"Are you okay with this?" Polite and cautious as ever, he checked in with her, only heightening her anticipation.

"Tommy, if you don't kiss me right now I'm going to—"

Fortunately, she never got to finish that threat.

As if exacting revenge for the silly nickname no one else

dared to use in reference to the tough garage owner, he wasn't quite gentle with her. His hunger was apparent when he first nibbled on her bottom lip, drawing it between his own before cursing then sealing his mouth over hers.

They bumped noses, a little awkward at first—rusty—until they found a rhythm that was uniquely theirs.

Her hands left her sides and reached upward, her fingers spearing into his short hair. She loved the way the silver of it glinted in the moonlight. When she drew him toward her, so she could return the teasing swipes of his tongue over her own, he sank lower bit by bit.

A moan escaped Willie as Tom covered her, deepening his kiss. Firm muscles squished her in the most pleasant way possible, flattening her breasts against his chest and the curve of her belly against his abs. The hard length of his cock impressed itself into her mound through the thin cotton they each wore. She shivered.

Lord, how she'd missed being with a man like this.

As if he could read her mind, his hand wandered up her side then flicked open the top button of her nightgown. Then the next…

His fingers slid inside and angled toward her breast, making her whimper even before he'd actually touched her.

"Is everything okay?" A knock came on the door.

Quinn!

Willie flew out from under Tom so fast she crashed onto the floor, leaving him sprawled flat on his face before leveling a wry grin at her. Not at all sorry, that scoundrel!

"Fine!" she shouted, though it emerged more like a squeak, really.

18

"Are you sure? It sounded as if someone was having nightmares." Quinn would know what that was like. Damn it. She'd probably woken him up with her distress then confused him with her moans. The last thing she needed was for him to worry. Family came first, for both her and Tom.

Speaking of, he grabbed the quilt and drew it over himself, plopping a pillow in his lap. Then he waved his fingers toward the door. So she made her way across the room and opened it.

A younger, more vulnerable version of Roman Daily, whom the kids called Barracuda because he drove one, stood there with his fingers balled in the sides of the sweatpants hanging off his too-damn-skinny hips.

Lying would be unacceptable when he confronted his own demons so bravely, letting them in more and more often to his own fears lately.

"You're right. I was dreaming about Steven." She quickly corrected herself. "My husband. The night he died."

"Do you want a hug, Ms. Brown?" Quinn nearly unraveled all the fine distraction Tom had granted her with that sweet offer, bringing tears rushing to her eyes.

"I would, yes." More though, she wanted to squeeze him in return for the heartache he'd already suffered at such a young age. "Thank you."

When they separated, he looked up at Tom. His eyes were full of questions. "Why weren't you making her feel better?"

Then they narrowed. He took in his surrogate dad, hiding beneath the blankets. His stare flickered to the undone buttons at the top of her gown.

"Wait. Were you two—?"

Tom didn't deny it. Neither did she.

"Ugh! Gross." Quinn morphed into the teenager he should have been instead of the survivor he'd been forced to be. Nothing could have made her happier than his mock-disgust right then. "Seriously? As if it isn't bad enough walking in on the Hot Rods making out all the damn time. Now I've got to worry about you two, too?"

"Watch your mouth." The automatic scold came out before she could even think about it.

"Damn is hardly a curse." He rolled his eyes. "Have you ever listened to what my brother and the rest of those guys say? *Heck*, Mustang Sally probably has the dirtiest mouth of anybody."

"That's true." Willie propped her hand on her hip. "I'll be sure to remind them about their foul language in the morning."

"Aw, man. Don't yell at them because of me." He groaned. "Not again."

"No one's in trouble." Tom laughed from the bed. "How about we make a deal? You're off the hook if you let us off it, too. Sorry we woke you up, son."

"Never mind." He waved off Tom's apology. "I'm going back to my room. To bed. Try to keep it down, would you? Better yet, I'm putting my headphones in. So if the house is burning down, someone come tell me."

He might have grumbled, but he couldn't disguise the hint of a smile turning his somber face into one tinged with mischief. No way would he keep this to himself. Willie mentally prepared herself for the hopeful questions her daughters would pepper her with tomorrow. They'd been nudging her toward Tom for months now.

"Goodnight, Quinn." Willie kissed him on the forehead, grinning as he walked away.

Then she returned to bed, not bothering with their ridiculous sheet safety zones anymore. Tom grinned as she curled up beside him, resting her cheek on his chest. Together, they laughed about getting busted fooling around and what their kids would think.

Mostly, they enjoyed knowing they'd both given themselves permission to find out where this thing between them might lead. Even if it was at their own pace, slower than one of the snails she'd spotted crossing a leaf in his garden yesterday as they'd swayed in his hammock, enjoying the fine weather and better company.

For the first time in twenty-one years, she forgot about her nightmares, replacing them with the joy of the present.

Maybe there was hope for her yet.

TWO

"hanks for coming." Tom opened the door wider and welcomed Rick Andersen, kickass private investigator, into his home.

"I thought we were going to quit meeting like this now that you've got your kids straightened out." The guy grinned as he slapped Tom on the back then headed for the kitchen table as if he lived there. Shit, he'd spent a hell of a lot of time hanging around, digging through details and plotting to protect the Hot Rods family. "The four-way wedding was fantastic, by the way."

"Thanks, Amber did a great job of planning it." Tom grinned. "You might need to get that tux ready again not too long from now. I think she and Gavyn are going to make a run of that forever thing for themselves someday. Hopefully soon, though I don't blame them for not rushing into it, considering everything they've got going on with his recovery and setting up Hot Rides."

He thought of the younger generation surrounding him and how fortunate they'd been in the love department. Sure, they'd had ups and downs, but they'd conquered their issues. He hoped that luck held now that it seemed like his turn.

"That's good news." Rick's smile dimmed a bit. "I was worried there for a while. You know, the morning after the ceremony, when he fell off the wagon. Happy to hear things are turning around for them. And you?"

"Well, I called you out here again, didn't I?" Tom grimaced.

"Yeah. Is it the senators? I know it's election time. Tell me they're not trying some shit with Rebel?"

"Nah, nothing like that, Bryce and Kae are fine." He shook his head.

"Another kid in trouble?" Rick's eyes widened. "Where the hell are you going to put this one? Bunk beds in Quinn's room?"

"That's not it either." He crossed his arms then twisted his neck one way then the other, cracking it to release the tension building there.

"I'm a detective, not a mind reader." The other guy laughed. "Come on, what's up?"

"I want to look into Willie's past." There. He'd said it.

"Whoa." Rick waved his hands in front of his chest. "Like snooping? I may be kind of sleazy when I need to blend into a bad neighborhood and dig up dirt, but I don't take on those kinds of cases. You know, like husbands trying to prove their wives are banging the guy's best friend or petty bullshit like that. If there's something you gotta know, you're going to have to man up and ask her about it yourself. Besides, I think she could hurt me if I pissed her off."

"How long have you known me?" Tom pressed his lips

together. He hated to get irritated, but this shit had him on edge in a way solving his family's problems never had before. "It's not like that. I've already talked to Willie about this situation. There are things *she* doesn't know. Couldn't figure out on her own."

"So why are you the one talking to me and not her?" The guy sat back in his chair, his eyes slightly squinted as he listened intently. A skill he excelled at. Tom would hate to have Rick as an enemy. The guy was a little more than half his age, street smart, tough, and committed to justice. It was a respectable combination.

"Because she gave up on finding out the truth a long time ago. Or maybe she made her mind up without all the facts and details. She's not over it, though." Tom shrugged. "I thought, maybe, if I give her definitive answers, she can finally let it go."

"We're talking about her dead husband, right?"

"Yeah," he confirmed. "This might be pointless. It was a long time ago, far away, and I doubt there's anything to be found."

"You leave that part to me." Rick cut him off before he could convince himself it was pointless to stir up old trouble. "I like Ms. Brown. And I think the two of you have something together even if you're too fucking stubborn to admit it. If this will help… Tell me more."

Tom waited until Rick hauled his cell phone out and opened the note-taking app he'd often used when they had these kinds of discussions in the past. When the guy was ready, he continued, "Her husband, Steven, died twenty-one years ago outside of McComb, Mississippi. Car accident. A really bad one."

"Shit." The investigator's brows drew together as he jotted down the facts.

"Yeah. Head-on collision with a delivery truck then through

the guardrails into a river. If he lived long enough, he drowned."

"Hell of a way to go." Rick shuddered. "But I don't get it, Tom. What am I supposed to look into here? Does she think he was drinking? Or maybe that he committed suicide by car wreck or something?"

"God, no." He waved off those horrid thoughts. "She suspects foul play. Actually, I should say she's convinced of it. And she believes it's her fault."

"What?" Rick's head whipped up at that, shooting Tom a that's-total-bullshit kind of stare that he had probably used himself when he first realized Willie's hang-ups.

"It's not exactly a hotbed of acceptance down there. She's black, he wasn't. People are fucking idiots." Tom shrugged. "They were threatened. Repeatedly. She says there were skid marks and eye-witness reports of a second car forcing her husband into oncoming traffic."

"Now *that's* a whole other story." Rick leaned toward Tom. The guy had a knack for this kind of work. He was definitely in the right line of business. When his interest was piqued, nothing could stop him from discovering the truth.

"No kidding." Tom leaned his back against the refrigerator and crossed his legs at the ankle. "I know it's been forever, but whoever did that to Willie, took her husband and those kids' dad… They deserve to pay for it."

"So you want revenge? Or just closure for your lady friend?" Rick didn't seem as if he'd mind either way.

"No reason we couldn't have both, I suppose. She's top priority. Always will be."

"You're a good guy, Tom London." Rick clicked a button on

the side of his phone, blackening the screen before he pocketed the device. "I think I have everything I'll need. It might take longer than usual, considering how far back I have to go to find people I can talk to who might know more."

"Fine. Whatever it takes. Usual fees?" Tom asked. Then he clarified, "Travel expenses on top of course if you need to go down there in person."

"Not this time. Consider it a frequent-customer discount. I'm taking this case because I think you deserve a chance at the happiness you've given so many other people around you." Rick stood. He crossed to Tom, who met him part of the way, and clapped him on the back, jarring him a bit. "If knowing this will allow you to go after Ms. Brown, or her to quit running from you, I'll do my best. Can't guarantee anything, but I'll see what I can do."

"That's really generous of you. I insist—"

"Nope." Rick shook his head and swaggered toward the door. "Who knows, maybe someday you can return the favor. Or you can have your kids spruce up my car some. We'll work it out."

"You want a drink out back before you head home or you have actual work to do today?" Tom enjoyed talking to the guy and he sensed a loneliness in Rick that he understood.

"Well, now I've got something to keep me busy." He smiled. "Thanks for the offer, though. I think I can get some calls in this afternoon while businesses are still open."

"I really appreciate this, Rick." Tom followed the other guy to the door and opened it wide.

On the other side, Eli, Roman, Carver, and Holden were eating up most of the free space on the porch. When the hell had they gotten so damn big? He supposed Eli took after him some, though all those tattoos made his muscles seem more intimidating than Tom's lean, cut build.

Nothing a few hundred crunches a day couldn't earn a man.

Tom would never admit it, but he'd even done jivamukti with Sabra a few times lately to improve his flexibility. Poor Willie, she wasn't going to know what hit her when he unleashed his full potential on her.

He grinned.

"What's that shit-eater for?" Carver laughed as he smacked Tom in the stomach with the back of his hand.

"Nothing, nothing." He shook his head.

"Hey, Rick." Roman put his hand out and shook with the investigator. "Everything okay? You're not here about my mother, are you? Nothing's changed, has it? She's still fine with us having Quinn. Right?"

Oh, shit. Tom hadn't meant to worry Barracuda. That was more talking from him than they usually heard in a week.

"Sure. Don't worry about that." Rick evaded the question, loyal to Tom as always. "Nobody's taking your brother away. You know we wouldn't let that happen."

"Damn straight," Carver—Roman's new husband—added. He put his hand on Roman's shoulder and squeezed. "Even if we have to kick an ass or two, he's staying with us as long as he wants."

"See you guys around." The investigator trotted down the stairs then toward his sleek black Mercedes before they could interrogate him further.

"Thank you!" Tom called.

With the coast clear, the handful of Hot Rods barreled past Tom, piling into the kitchen. Was it any wonder he liked to sit outside when they occupied so much damn space? He remembered them as scrawny teenagers and shook his head over the men they'd grown into.

"Thought we'd come over and bug you for a while." Holden went straight to the pantry and hauled out the box of cookies Tom always kept on hand before popping a couple in his mouth. They weren't nearly as good as the ones his wife used to make Eli. It was a habit he hadn't been able to shake once she was gone, though. Maybe eating them reminded him of her and how sweet she'd been.

On occasion the guys would pop over for a beer out back. Not with Roman in tow, though. They didn't keep alcohol in their own apartment above the garage for his sake, and they certainly wouldn't crack open a cold one in front of him either. Not that he would probably mind anymore. He was pretty amazing in that regard.

Gavyn, on the other hand, they were even more careful around after his disastrous relapse into alcoholism several months ago. He was fighting, harder now than ever before, and none of the guys would make his journey tougher than it needed to be.

"Why? Ambrose crying again?" Tom laughed.

"How can such a tiny person make so much noise?" Carver wondered.

"And so much poop," Roman chimed in.

"Yeah, I thought Rebel was bad. Or Buster McHightops." Eli referred to one of the mechanics, Bryce, and the shop's puppy, which they shared joint custody of, though the Boston terrier had taken to sticking with Quinn most of the time lately. "That baby beats them all."

"You love her anyway." Tom could see right through their act. They might bitch and moan, but they were guys who cared for each other as strongly as their own soul mates. Together, they'd survived some unbelievable heartache, and it had made them inseparable. Kaige and Nola's baby might as well have been their own. They would protect her with their lives if needed. Tom had raised them right.

"And speaking of *luuuurve...*" Eli winked.

Oh shit, how had he forgotten?

Tom glanced at the clock. Yep, Quinn had gotten home from school about a half hour ago. There was no way he'd waited that long to spill what he'd seen the night before to his big brothers.

"We think you know something about that." Holden grinned.

"Wipe the crumbs off your face, son, and maybe I can take you a little more seriously." Tom put Swinger in his place. Or at least he tried.

"So you and Ms. Brown finally..." Carver wiggled his brows.

"No, nothing happened. It wouldn't have even if Quinn hadn't interrupted. We're taking things slow." He shrugged.

"If you went any damn slower you'd be going backwards," Carver teased. "Hell, in the past year Kaige met Nola, fell in love, knocked her up, got married, and had a kid. Okay, so they sort of jumbled things up there with the oopsie baby part. All's well that ends well though, right? Meanwhile, I bet you haven't even gotten to second base with Ms. Brown."

Tom remembered how damn close his fingers had been to

cupping her breast the night before. They flexed as he imagined it wouldn't be long now. Hopefully it didn't take another year to get a hell of a lot further than that. Still, he would wait if it did.

"Meep! Shut the hell up. I don't want to think about Ms. Brown's tits or my dad getting to second base with anyone, for that matter." Eli rubbed the lines that appeared between his eyes.

"Welcome to my world." Tom snorted. "How many times do I have to break out the secret knock when I visit over there then pretend like I don't hear the moaning and whatnot before we act like I didn't almost barge in on some of you doing God-knows-what to each other in that living room? Remind me never to sit on your furniture again."

"That's probably a good call." Roman nodded.

"Besides, I'm pretty sure both Nola and Amber will smash your balls for talking about their mom like that," Holden warned. "I will laugh my ass off at the sight of their vengeance, too. Well, actually, Nola's pretty hot when she's pissed. I might get other ideas…"

"That's what I'm talking about. Right there. All right, that's enough for me." Tom shook his head. "Why don't we call a truce? You don't worry about my love life and I won't mess around with yours. I was scheduled to babysit this weekend so you could have the apartment to yourselves for a while, but I might feel a cold coming on."

He pretended to clear his throat.

The gang had a complex relationship, one that involved each of them in some way or another. He knew they had sex outside their committed couplings or trios, sharing partners within the group—especially the guys with the other guys. As for the

31

details, he didn't need to know exactly how they expressed their bond with each other. As long as everyone agreed to the system and it worked for them, he was supportive.

He'd never turn his back on them. Besides, Ambrose was adorable. He thought he might enjoy being a grandparent even more than he'd relished being a dad. Considering these kids had saved him from losing his mind with grief, that was really saying something.

"Okay, okay!" Eli held his hand up, palm out. "That's not playing fair."

"That's what I thought." Tom smirked.

"Can I just say one more thing?" Carver asked.

"I'm pretty sure I can't stop you. You've got a big mouth." He elbowed the smaller guy in his side.

"Yes. Yes, he does." Roman shot his husband a secret smile that had them all groaning.

"What did we *just* talk about?" Tom rubbed his eyes with the thumb and forefinger of one hand.

"Right. So. I'm going to leave it at this… If you were one of us, and we were you, you'd be giving us hell for not going after what's right there in front of our faces. Ms. Brown is awesome and you two are even awesomer together."

"That's not even a word." Eli shook his head.

"Whatever. I'm not as good at this as Tom is." Carver held his hand out and Roman took it, lending him strength. "What I mean, is that…you should go for it."

"Not that it's really any of you kids' business—"

"Fuck that, Tom." Roman laughed this time. "Everything around here is your business. And you're ours."

"—but I'm planning on it." Tom smiled. "I already told her I'm gonna wait her out."

"Is 'her' my mom?" Amber asked as she joined them, with her boyfriend and business partner, Gavyn, right behind.

"Ummm..." Tom wasn't sure how to respond.

"I really hope it is." She came over and kissed his burning cheek. "Except, I came over here to say I don't think you should waste any more time."

"You've waited long enough, haven't you, Tom?" Gavyn asked. "Everyone can see you're great together."

"What is this bullshit?" Tom threw his hands up. "Gang Up on Tom Day?"

"Or, as Ms. Brown might say...Gang Up on *Tooooommmmmy* Day," Eli teased in a high-pitched singsong.

Each of the kids cracked up at that.

"All right. That's enough. I can manage my own affairs, thank you," he blustered.

"So you admit there is an affair to manage?" Holden prodded.

"Look, I don't know what you call it these days. There's something there, yes. Now, if you don't leave me alone you'll drive me crazy and then no one will be getting any. I'll be locked up, Willie will be sad—I think—and you'll be on babysitting duty for the rest of your lives." He shot them the I'm-the-dad-don't-argue glare that had never really worked much on the gang of streetwise kids, less so since they'd become independent adults.

"I see how it is. You can dish out advice, for years and years, but you're not very good at taking it, are you? *Tommy?*" Holden grinned.

"That's it. I'm hiding those cookies," Tom threatened.

"Not if I eat them first." Swinger grinned then stole another handful.

"Careful there, buddy," Gavyn teased him. "Sugar is addicting, too. Besides, you wouldn't want to get soft around the middle for your girl, now would you? Her arms are so defined from that crazy yoga stuff she could probably smash those cookies with her guns."

"I'm never soft for Sabra." Holden smirked.

Tom gave up. He put his head in his hand and let them faux-fight with a shit ton of sexual innuendo thrown in. If he smiled to himself, content with how settled and comfortable they were in their own unique and colorfully inked skins, that was for him alone to know.

Maybe they had a point.

It hadn't been easy for any of them to trust after being screwed over by life. They had faith in themselves, their partners, and the encouragement he'd given them.

Tom owed them the same.

After all, Willie had become like a mom to them, something almost none of them had had growing up. Or at least, not in a positive way.

Bringing her into their family, permanently, wouldn't only be best for him.

It'd benefit his kids, too.

And he'd do anything for them.

Such a sacrifice. He laughed at himself as he enjoyed the ruckus they caused around him.

THREE

Willie grabbed the stack of mail out of her box then went inside the house she'd shared with her daughters. Both had moved out within months of each other. She wished them well on the next phase of their lives, with fine young men who'd fought to overcome adversity. Not to mention Nola's little one.

Still, as she looked around their living room she noticed the brighter squares on the faded paint, where pictures had previously hung on the walls. Her daughters had taken some to decorate their new places. No laughter, or arguing, or blaring TVs interrupted the absolute silence. A light coating of dust hazed the coffee table since none of them had been there lately to either clean it or make marks in the film.

A cramped though lively house had turned into a museum seemingly overnight.

Her girls were headed in the right direction. That didn't

mean she didn't worry about them. Amber, who was coping with Gavyn's addiction and helping him successfully navigate staying clean while launching a business. Nola, with the baby, her recent marriage, and figuring out her place at Hot Rods.

It was a lot to handle even before Willie got to thinking about herself and Tom London.

The slew of recent changes had her head spinning. At least that's what she thought it was. She wandered over to the couch and sank onto it, pressing her hands to her face to ward off the throbbing that began again behind her eyes. It'd been happening more and more frequently lately. Her nightmares had been growing more vicious, too.

After years of battling anxiety and depression after Steven's death, she recognized the symptoms of an imminent rough period. So she did what she'd been putting off.

Willie took her phone from her purse then selected her doctor's contact.

The woman who answered was new, since the previous assistant had retired recently.

"Yes, I'm a patient of Dr. Smith. I'd like to get a refill on some of my anti-anxiety medication." She hated to admit she needed it, but it was the responsible thing to do. Coping had become so much easier once she'd been appropriately diagnosed and treated. Though she didn't always need the help, she figured she could use it now. For a while, until things settled down again.

"I'm sorry, ma'am. That prescription is expired," the woman informed her cheerily. "I can make an appointment for you to see the doctor if you'd like."

It was never a rigorous deal. A few questions, some blood work, then bing, bam, boom, she was out of there. So she agreed.

After what sounded like a few thousand keystrokes, the woman perked up even more, if that was possible. "Actually, it looks like Dr. Smith has had a cancellation for tomorrow afternoon if you'd like to sneak in then."

"Sure, that sounds terrific." Well, not really. She didn't particularly enjoy going to the doctor. At least it would be over and done with soon. Especially since she could only imagine how much more determined and forward Tom would be now that he'd declared open war on their friend status.

Willie spent some time dusting the living room and chucked a bunch of the food that had spoiled in the fridge then took out the garbage. She had the place shined up by the time she stood and surveyed the tiny house that had been their home for so long.

Would it be her place for much longer?

It both terrified and thrilled her that she didn't think so.

Her heart had already defected to Team London.

Spur of the moment, she picked up her phone again and tapped the picture of Tommy grinning at her. She'd snapped it while she sat beside him at the Hot Rods quadruple wedding. He looked so damn handsome, and so happy, that she couldn't help but grin in return. It also made what she was about to do harder. She had to be sure.

"Hey there, Ms. Brown." His warm greeting nearly melted her resolve. "What time can I expect you home? Want me to cook up some of my famous spaghetti?"

She hated to tell him that his sauce was kind of bland and yet, somehow, simultaneously too salty. So she didn't, happily eating it when he went through the trouble to prepare it for her.

"Actually, Tommy..."

"Oh, no." He groaned. "I know that tone. Just say it fast. You changed your mind about what we talked about last night? You're not that into me. What?"

"I just need a night to myself." She swallowed. Her eyes stung as they filled with unexpected tears. "To be sure, you know? I want to think everything over before we do something rash."

"Honey, the very *last* thing we've been is hasty." He chuckled. "Trust me, the kids were over before, practically offering to donate their stash of condoms to us."

"Oh jeez." Her fingers flew to cover her open mouth. "They weren't."

"Sure were. But it's your choice, not theirs. So take all the time you need. I'll be right here when you're ready." He sounded disappointed yet understanding as ever. What had she done to deserve someone like him?

"Okay." She hated that despite her yearning to rush back to his house and into his arms, she couldn't allow herself to do it yet. "Tomorrow, I promise."

"I'll miss you tonight," he murmured, setting her insides on fire. Kindling a flame she hadn't fanned in years.

"Same goes." It wasn't a lie either.

"If you have a nightmare or want to talk…about anything… call. Doesn't matter what time it is, you understand?" His firm tone only turned her on more.

"Yes, Tommy." She tried not to giggle, knowing how much he despised her nickname for him. It was so inappropriate for a man like him it made her grin every time she whipped it out. Failing to stifle her amusement, a hint of her laughter seeped through.

"Don't tempt me to make you scream my name. The real

one. I bet I can make you do it, you know?" His husky guarantee was doing nothing to fortify her will. She had to cut this off before she flew back to him and begged him to make good on his promises. "I may be out of practice, but I'm willing to spend some quality time relearning how to do it right."

"Seriously? Phone sex now, too?" Quinn's groan came through loud and clear over the phone. "I'm going to the garage!"

"Be back in an hour for dinner," Tom told the kid.

In the background, Quinn agreed. Poor bastard would have to suffer and eat that pasta. He would never complain. Tomorrow, she'd make it up to him with his favorite, her home-cooked meatloaf with fresh-baked berry pie.

Considering she wasn't on site to be mortified about the interruption, Willie allowed herself to rock with peals of laughter.

"Such a pretty sound." Tom sighed after the slamming door signaled Quinn's departure. "Are you sure about this?"

"Just one night. To get myself ready."

"You're everything I want, Willie. Exactly like you are." His grin practically rang through his voice. "Unless you're waxing your legs or some shit tonight."

Ah, crap. She had to remember to shave, too?

This intimacy thing was harder than she remembered.

"Very funny," she sniffed. "Goodnight, Tommy."

"Sleep well, Willie."

Somehow she knew she wouldn't doze even half as well as when he was by her side. Maybe that was the last shred of proof she needed to dive into a relationship with him.

Who was she kidding? They'd been dating for months already.

Hours later, as she tossed and turned, she was one-hundred-percent certain this was no longer her place in the world. Whether she'd intended to or not, she'd moved on...and into Tom London's life.

She hoped they were both ready for what came next.

Before the sun had risen the following morning, she turned off the lights, smiled at the empty interior of her house, and headed back to Hot Rods. It felt as if she was going in the right direction. The night alone had given her plenty of time to think and gain perspective. This was the best thing to do.

When she got there, she knocked on the door to Tom's house, although she had a key in her purse. It still seemed polite. To her surprise, it was Quinn who answered.

"Sorry, Ms. Brown," he said. "Tom's not home."

"Oh." She hated the disappointment zinging through her. She'd only been away for a single evening and already she was having withdrawals. What would it do to her if something—heaven forbid—happened to him? How would she cope again?

"He went for a jog with Carver." Quinn grinned. "He was mumbling about having to get in better shape when he left."

"If that man was any more ripped..." She trailed off, realizing just how inappropriate her audible thoughts had been about to get. It would have been impossible to miss the hardness of his body when he'd held her the other night or when he'd hovered over her, kissing the stuffing out of her afterward.

"I gotta get ready for school," Quinn shouted as he ran upstairs, probably to claim his backpack. He'd been very diligent

40

about his homework and grades since Alanso had promised to teach him more about tuning bikes while working part-time at Hot Rides if he did well in his classes. "Gavyn is taking me on his motorcycle!"

Each of the Hot Rods had pitched in to welcome Quinn and give him every opportunity they'd missed out on until coming there themselves. How could she not love every single one of them?

"Did you eat breakfast?" she called to him.

"Yep, cereal with some of the fresh fruit you cut up mixed in." He smiled. "I even packed myself a sandwich for lunch. Tom offered me the leftover spaghetti. I was really generous. I told him we'd better save it for you since you missed out last night."

Willie clutched her stomach as she laughed. "You stinker."

"Hey, I took one for the team last night. Your turn." He hugged her quickly then said, "See you later."

When he hesitated at the door, she asked, "Everything okay?"

"You *are* going to be here when I get home today, right?"

"Absolutely." She crossed to the teenager and squeezed him tight. Only for a moment, though hopefully enough to reassure him. He seemed so tough, but he was still finding his way here.

"Okay, good. Gotta go!"

Willie washed the few dishes left in the sink, dried them, and put them away. She peeked into the cabinets and drew up a shopping list. She could swing by and pick up the rest of what she needed for dinner after her doctor's appointment.

When eight o'clock rolled around and Tom still wasn't home, she tried not to panic.

On a piece of paper, she wrote a note.

I'm over with the girls. Nola's going out this morning. Probably will be done babysitting around lunchtime. ~Willie

She'd crossed to the door before something came over her and she rushed back, adding a couple hearts to the note. Beneath her name, she put, *PS... I shaved more than my legs, and I'm wearing fancy underpants. Want to see?*

Before she could change her mind and rip up the proof of her insanity, she dashed out the door and across the lot to the metal stairway leading to the expansive apartment over the Hot Rods garage. It had to be huge to house the eight mechanics as well as their significant others, with room to spare for a nursery.

She knocked and waited for Nola to open the door, just in case there were any last-minute shenanigans going on before the mechanics went to work at their famous restoration shop downstairs. Instead, it was her other daughter, Amber, who greeted her.

"Hey, baby." Willie hugged her tight. "I wasn't expecting to see you this morning. This is a nice surprise."

"I figured I'd keep Nola company while she's relaxing at the spa." She shrugged one shoulder. "Actually, Gavyn kind of insisted. We've been going nuts with the planning for Hot Rides' grand opening on top of my regular events. He wants me to take some time off and chill out."

"Sounds like a good idea. A few hours won't kill you, and you'll be even more effective once you're refreshed." Her daughter was helping her boyfriend launch a sister-shop to Hot Rods. It would focus on building custom choppers like the one he rode. Between the notoriety of the restomod business downstairs, Gavyn's expertise, exposure on the reality TV show that featured the mechanics, and her daughter's business sense,

Willie knew they'd be a smashing success.

"Besides…" Nola motioned her over to the couch, where she was nursing Ambrose. "We kind of wanted to talk to you about something."

The hair on Willie's neck rose as she realized they'd conned her.

"Is this some kind of intervention?" She knew her daughters well.

"Not exactly," Amber said, though she looked awfully guilty.

"Start talking then." She tapped her lips with her index finger.

"I guess we were surprised to hear the guys joking around with Eli yesterday. They said that you and Tom haven't…you know." Nola peeked up at her mom. "Is that true?"

"Not that it's your concern, but, yes. That's right." Willie attempted to act as if it was no big deal. Inside she was freaking out. Honestly, her girls had a hell of a lot more experience than she did recently in the bedroom department.

"Well, I guess we wanted to say that if it was us balking like that, you'd slap some sense into us." Amber huffed. "What was all that, 'it's okay to be scared, Amber' nonsense you preached to me when I was afraid to commit to Gavyn? You told me I had to have faith in the people I loved. Did you mean *any* of that?"

"For you, yes." She crossed her arms.

"What's good for the Amber is good for the Willie," Nola said then wrinkled her nose. "That didn't come out how I meant it."

"Ack," Amber agreed. "This is hard enough without thinking about…willies."

"Why don't you save us some prolonged discussion then?

43

Say what you want to say." Willie had always been open and honest with her daughters. Especially about their bodies as they matured. She never wanted them to be ashamed or make ignorant decisions. Looked like she might have excelled there, since Nola had chosen a polyamorous lifestyle.

"Fine." Nola, always the less patient of the two, blurted, "Have you done it since Daddy died?"

"Child, hush!" she gasped. Had her own daughter just asked her if she was practically a born-again virgin?

"Oh my God! You're right, Nola." Amber's eyes widened as she glanced to her sister then back to Willie. "She hasn't.

"Is that why you're freaking out so much? Is that why you hid at home last night?" Nola didn't relent. "Because you're scared of having sex again?"

Why the hell hadn't she gotten that prescription refilled sooner, Willie wondered as she tried—only partially successfully—not to hyperventilate.

"There's nothing to worry about, Momma." Amber tried to calm her down.

"Yeah. You're for sure a MILF," Nola declared. "Or GILF, I guess."

"Do I even want to know what that means?" she asked ruefully.

"Uh, probably not." Amber cut her sister off. "Don't worry. It's a good thing. It means you're hot. This isn't going to be an issue for you. Tom is one of the sexiest older guys I've ever seen, and he's totally into you. Do what comes naturally, that's all."

"Just do it." Nola nodded. "*Him.* Do him. Put the man out of his misery already, would you?"

"It's got to be like riding a bike, right?" Willie speculated aloud when she finally found her voice again.

Both of her daughters cracked up so hard that Ambrose fidgeted in her post-milk slumber.

"What?" Willie shrugged.

"I think riding Tom London will be a hell of a lot more exciting!" Nola cried.

Amber snorted. "Now all I can think of is Maria Von Trapp and her huge bicycle getting it on with him. Thanks a lot."

"I'd cut that bitch if she dared," Willie said just to make the pair of them laugh some more. Her heart soared, seeing them happy, sharing in their delight.

There'd been too many times in her younger years when she hadn't been able to enjoy the simple pleasures, either because there'd been nothing to laugh about or because she hadn't escaped the fog of depression long enough to join in.

"So you're going for it?" Nola's eyes sparkled.

"I think so." She tried not to wince when they gave each other a high-five. "For your information, I'd already decided that last night. Thanks for the pep talk, anyway."

Amber rushed over to hug her, only letting go when Nola butted in for a squeeze of her own, transferring Ambrose to her in the process. "We're happy for you, Momma."

"You deserve this," Amber added. The sheen of tears in their eyes would have Willie bawling if she didn't shoo them soon.

"Well, now that you got me psyched, you'd better hurry the hell up so that you get back here on time!" she whisper-shouted at the girls as they gathered their purses and car keys to keep from startling her precious granddaughter. "I'm not getting any younger, you know?"

"Ew, Momma. Gross." Amber winked at her.

FOUR

Willie spent the next four hours doting on Ambrose, folding laundry, and baking cookies while thinking of the young couples hard at work building their futures in the garage beneath her. Anticipation began to outweigh the nervous flutters in her tummy as her speculation drifted repeatedly to the man who'd started it all, and what he'd be like in bed.

Somehow she figured he'd be less polite and rawer than Steven had ever been with her. She hoped he didn't filter his primal side, leaving her with a shadow of the things she adored about him. His fierceness reassured her that he could, and would, protect his family at any cost. It was maybe the single most attractive thing about the man.

No longer delicate, she didn't want to be treated like she was.

Surprisingly, when noon rolled around and the girls

returned, looking more gorgeous than ever with their hair and nails done, Tom hadn't made an appearance.

Was he waiting for her to come to him?

Probably, considering how she'd fled from him yesterday.

Nola rushed over to her and scooped Ambrose to her bosom. For her first time away from the baby, she'd done great. Willie remembered too well how hard it was to let go. Almost as hard as it was to let someone in again.

"Well, what are you waiting for?" They practically shoved her out the door.

She wished she'd taken the time for some beauty appointments of her own when hugging each of her children goodbye and thanking them silently for the kick in the pants. Tom would have to take her as she was. Or not.

The possibility of rejection hadn't even entered her imagination until then.

He wouldn't do that to her, would he?

Everyone was entitled to change their mind. Still, it might kill her if he did now.

Willie darted across the lawn and rushed into his house without knocking. She wasn't sure when it had started to feel like her home too, but she could no longer deny that it did.

Tom sat at the table, reading the paper.

He took one look at her bright eyes and the shadows her hard nipples cast on her floral sundress then grinned. Carefully, he folded the newsprint then set it aside before crossing to her in a couple of his superhuman strides. "I like this look on you, Willie."

"Desperation?"

"If that's what you want to call it, sure." He didn't mess around, lowering his head and planting a juicy welcome kiss on her lips. His hands cupped her hips, keeping her still as he plundered. "I prefer primed. Seductive."

She thought that implied a lot more grace than she possessed at the moment, but she didn't feel like wasting time to discuss it. Not anymore.

Ready for action, she flung her arms around him and practically climbed his body as she tried to return his kiss.

"Give me five seconds, honey." He breathed hard as he separated them. "I don't want anyone ruining our fun this time."

A flick of his wrist shut the door behind her and locked it. Then he jammed a chair beneath the door handle and even drew the curtains. "Just in case."

Willie appreciated the insurance. She certainly didn't need an audience for her artless fumbling. It would be humiliating enough when he discovered her limited experience.

Tom stalked closer, backing her against the kitchen wall. He gathered her hair in one hand then began to feast on the column of her neck, making her purr.

"Tommy?" she whispered.

"Yeah." He didn't stop his maddening kisses, licks, and love bites. The sparkling desire he infused into her bloodstream with every passing second distracted her, eroding her ability to do anything except say it like it was.

"I'm nervous."

"Me too, honey." He collected her, drawing her close enough that she couldn't deny how damn hard he was for her. "Why don't we take the edge off? So we're both more relaxed."

"Can I touch you?" she asked softly.

He groaned. "Anytime you want."

"Will you tell me if I'm doing it right?" She bit her lip at how untested she sounded…because she was.

"I'm pretty sure it will be obvious." He licked along her collarbone with sweeps of his warm, skilled tongue.

"Time out." She wasn't sure which of them was more disappointed when he lifted his head to meet her stare. "What I'm trying to say here…"

"You're going to have to spell it out for me, Willie." He grinned. "My brain is a few pints low on blood at the moment."

"I haven't been with a man in twenty-one years. And then only Steven. We were both young. Exclusive. Virgins when we met as kids." She shook her head, scrunching her eyes closed. "I have pretty much no experience that counts. If I had to fill out a sex resume to make love with you, I'd be unhireable."

"Good thing you never secretly aspired to be a prostitute then, huh?" He peppered her parted lips with soft kisses. "I'm more than willing to train you for the job, Willie."

She shivered in his hold.

Then he paused. "You know I haven't slept with anyone since Michelle either, right? Thirteen years for me. Though I certainly wasn't a saint before I fell for her."

"Seriously?"

"Yeah, I fucked my way through half of Middletown in my younger days." He grinned.

"Not that. You pig." She swatted at his bulging arm, laughing where a moment ago she'd been on the verge of panicky tears. "You really haven't…?"

"Me and my hand have gotten awfully friendly. That's about

the extent of it." He frowned. "Like I said, I fooled around plenty before I was married. After… Well, it just didn't seem very appetizing to do it with someone I didn't love."

"Plus there were the kids to take care of." She supplied for him, unsure which of them she referred to. Both, she supposed.

"A business to run. The shelter to think of. Paying bills and a whole lot of tedious shit I'd never had to do before. I was angry at the world, not fit for company anyway. I worked out a lot when I had extra energy. Nothing fancy like the kids do at the gym these days, but I've probably done a million pushups in my life." He scrubbed a hand through his short hair, making the results of his decade of exercise even more noticeable. "Son of a bitch, Willie. I wasn't that worried. I mean, it's gotta be like riding a bike, right?"

"That's what I said!" She giggled, pausing only to kiss him a few more times before things turned serious once more.

"So we'll go slowly, with training wheels." He took her hand and led her into the living room. He closed the curtains there too, dimming the sunlight and reminding her of the night they had spent together. "I want you to be comfortable with this. With me. If touching me is what you want, that's where we'll start."

He didn't hesitate when he peeled his shirt over his head, revealing the washboard abs and defined lines of his arms. She'd seen his bare chest and the muscles rippling in his shoulders plenty before, while he worked around the yard, or tinkered with one of the projects the Hot Rods had at the garage. The sight never failed to impress her.

This time she had his permission to explore with more than her greedy stare.

She approached him cautiously, afraid of overloading her senses.

Without once looking away from her, he took her hands in his and lifted them to his mouth, kissing her knuckles lightly before pressing her palms to his pecs. She kneaded them as she leaned forward for a gentle kiss, loving how his heartbeat quickened against her palm when their lips met and glided across each other.

"You smell good," he murmured against her mouth when they paused to catch their breath. "Like cinnamon."

"I baked snickerdoodles while I was babysitting this morning." She smiled at him. He did have a sweet tooth.

"I would normally pout, seeing as you didn't bring me any." He sipped from her lips again, making her eyelids lower despite the powerful pull she felt to fall into his stare. "I'm only hungry for one thing right now, though. I've got to taste you soon, Willie."

She grinned. "Going slow didn't last long, did it?"

He laughed. "Sorry, I can't help it that you're beautiful, tough, and fun to hang around. Being in the same room as you is enough to turn me on. That doesn't mean we have to rush. Here, I'll let you do whatever you want to me. That's what you wanted, isn't it?"

"Yes," she hummed when he popped the button on his jeans then tugged down the zipper, sighing in relief as he released the pressure on his hard-on.

"Mind if I lose these?" He glanced up at her.

The band of his underwear peeked through the gap in his pants, making her wish she had x-ray vision. She licked her lips. "Take them off, Tommy."

"Yes, ma'am." With a single swipe of his hands, he tucked his thumbs into the waist then shed his jeans and the cotton briefs beneath. He kicked them off his bare feet and stood before her, completely nude except for his watch, a leather cuff he sometimes wore on the opposite wrist, and his necklace.

Glorious, he could have been a statue in a fancy art museum, though she'd never seen a masterpiece as enticing as him before. She scanned up from his toned calves to his lightly furred thighs, gasping when her stare landed on his long, thick cock.

Maybe her memory was fuzzy, but she was pretty sure Steven had never looked like that. She whispered, "I'm not sure if I should be impressed, or scared."

Tom laughed, clearly enjoying the compliment underlying her apprehension.

He tugged her to him, tipping her chin up with one hand so she could see the excitement in his bright blue eyes. "This is what you do to me. A lot of women have tried, but none of them made me consider breaking my cold streak to fool around with them. I think you should be proud of yourself."

Thinking of things in that way filled her with courage. Made her bold, too.

"Lie down," she ordered, though it was really more like begging.

He allowed her to maintain her illusion of control. They both knew he could overpower her in an instant if he wanted. Worse, if he wrested control from her, she would probably surrender to his assertiveness and enjoy every second. This one time, it helped to feel as if she was running the show.

So he did as she commanded.

He shrugged then climbed onto the sofa, reclining with

one arm behind his head, propping himself up enough to keep watching her as she knelt beside him.

A long leg stretched the length of the couch, his bare foot sticking out over the end while his other one stayed planted on the ground, his toes curling into the carpet. She couldn't help herself. Reaching to the right, she encircled as much of his ankle as she could with her fingers, massaging the joint before gliding up to his knee, then along his quad to his narrow hip.

"I want to learn all of you like this." She hummed in appreciation as her other hand traveled from his shoulder to his ribs. They both laughed when he flinched at a ticklish spot. It might not have been suave or seductive, but each time she tested his flesh with the palm of her hand on some part of him—belly, neck, flank—he arched toward her touch.

Of course she kept getting distracted by his lush mouth, returning to sample his kisses over and over in between petting his magnificent body. When she traced the single tattoo he had, an armband on his right biceps that showcased the Hot Rods logo in the center, he sighed. "Yeah, the kids talked me into trying it. I never got hooked on it like them, though. One is enough for me."

"I like it." She smiled then pressed a quick kiss over the symbol. "It's fitting that Hot Rods is part of you, permanently. This place and the kids you raised. You have no idea how much I admire you. How strong you are to have gone on like you did."

"You survived too, Willie."

"Not as well as you." She refused to let her sadness seep into this moment, instead returning to her handiwork.

When she swept up to his shoulder then along his collarbone, her finger snagged on the chain he always kept around his neck.

"Ah, shit." He groaned. "Sorry. I don't even think about it being there anymore. Do you want me to take that off? You know, when we're like this. Or even always. If it bothers you—"

"No." Willie patted the wedding ring he'd kept close to his heart all these years. "You have it exactly right. It's simply part of you. I don't expect you to deny the past because you and I have this thing going on now. Or to make me forget what I've gone through before finding you. Our hearts are big enough for both, don't you think?"

She'd never had a wedding ring; they'd been too poor for that. If she had, she likely would have done the same. In any case, her soul still remembered the promises she'd made to Steven—and fulfilled, until death had they parted—though she had plenty of love left over to shower on Tom. Desire too, apparently.

"Yours certainly is." He wrapped his fingers carefully around the back of her neck, urging her closer so he could taste her again. "I'm not trying to replace Steven, honey. I only want to give you what I can in addition."

"It looks like that's a hell of a lot." She peeked down at the shaft lying heavy on his abdomen then back up at him, hoping to break the tension.

This should be fun, about pleasure only, none of the heartbreak they'd both suffered enough of already.

"Why don't you find out?" His brows rose hopefully as he clasped her hand and guided it down his center inch by inch. "I'm a patient man, but even I have limits. Would you mind checking me out a little farther south?"

"I didn't mean to tease you." It simply was impossible not to be in awe of every inch of him as she read each dip and curve of his chest, abs, and even his belly button, like Braille that spelled S-E-X-Y.

"It's okay. It's a sweet torture." He leveled a smoking-hot stare at her. "It's just that I'm weaker than I'd like to be with you so close to making my dreams come true."

"You've imagined this?" she asked, a hint of coyness in her tone.

"God, yes," he groaned. "A million times. I'm not going to lie, Willie. I've jacked off to thoughts of you so often it's a wonder I don't have calluses on my dick."

Why did that thought turn her on? If only she could have seen him!

"In your fantasy, what did I do to you?" she wondered.

"You were baking in the kitchen with only your apron on," he groaned. "I was lying here watching TV and checking out your ass."

Willie couldn't help it, she burst out laughing. "You really are a man, you know that?"

"I thought it was obvious." He stared at his cock and her fingers, which lingered close enough to brush the flared head if he so much as sneezed. "When you came to deliver me some treats, you realized I was hard for you. Just like this."

"What did I do about it?" she asked.

"You came over here, and knelt, exactly as you are now, then took me in your hand." As he spoke, he curled the fingers of her left hand around his shaft.

They gasped in unison.

He was so firm and hot in her clutch.

"Son of a bitch!" Tom threw his head back. "Your skin is so soft on me. Nothing like my fist when I stroked myself as I imagined you cupping my balls in your other hand."

She improvised, not only slipping her right hand between his thighs to weigh his heavy testicles, but also leaning in so her breath washed over the head of his ultra-stiff erection. Guessing where his imagination had taken this scenario, she began to pump him lightly as she kissed and licked his flat abdomen beside his hard-on.

It might have been new for her, but she found she loved drawing out their encounter and having him longing for her attention.

"You can hold me tighter, Willie." He demonstrated the perfect amount of pressure for him by covering her hand and tightening her grip on his cock. When she reached the top of her next stroke, a drop of pre-come trickled from the slit there, tempting her to lick it.

Having him stretched out before her, under the spell of the arousal she kindled in him, while she was still fully clothed and entirely in control did a lot to ease her nerves. There was no way she could deny that he needed her every bit as much as she'd come to need him.

Strong, yet utterly vulnerable, he showed her that it might be safe for her to follow suit. She rewarded his bravery by rolling his sac in her palm while increasing the pace of her stroking on his cock. The veins there stood out in relief, making the textured surface even more interesting to feel and study.

"When you look at me like that, I could come in seconds."

"I'd like to see that." A tiny smile flickered at the edges of her mouth when he groaned and jerked in her hold, making her fairly certain she would get her wish sooner rather than later.

His chest rose and fell now with his labored breathing.

Knowing she could affect him so intensely empowered her.

Willie tested out different ways of clutching him, rippling her fingers along his shaft when he cried out and cursed in response to her experimentation. She pumped him faster, then slower, then faster again, finding the pattern that made him plump in her fist.

When his hand buried in her hair and he urged her to lean over him, she knew he was beyond speaking. He'd gone to a place where actions communicated far more in any case.

She obliged him by nuzzling his balls and the base of his shaft before allowing her tongue to sneak out and lick him tentatively.

He groaned so loudly at the contact that she flinched, removing her mouth from him temporarily. The reassuring smile she thought he attempted looked more like a grimace of pain.

"Too much?" she asked. Hypersensitive after years of disuse, she could relate.

Even the soft lace of her bra rasped against her pebbled nipples right then.

For the first time, she couldn't wait for their roles to be reversed. Not a hint of trepidation remained. It was going to be spectacular when he finally fucked her.

"Not enough." He shook his head as he responded through clenched teeth. "Won't take a hell of a lot more, Willie. I want to come for you. Show you what you do to me."

That was fine by her.

She returned to where her fingers met his cock and rubbed her parted lips across the section of his shaft that protruded from her grip. Nibbling her way upward, she gave in to her wild urges and sampled the droplet of pearly fluid at his tip.

Tom groaned and called her name.

The ragged way he said it clued her in. If she didn't hurry, she'd be waiting to taste him until next time they played like this. Suddenly, she didn't want to delay any longer.

Willie took an inch or two of his length into her mouth while continuing the circuit of her left hand and the gentle massage of her right one. Her confidence soared when Tom grunted and lifted his hips from the couch, feeding more of himself to her.

The pressure of his head against her tongue made her choke a little. Still, she followed when he tried to retreat, giving her space to adjust. That wasn't what she wanted anymore.

Syncing the motion of her hand and mouth, she sucked his tip while her fingers worked at the root of his dick. It seemed he had plenty for both. Certain now, she realized Steven had never posed that much of a challenge to her gag reflex.

When she swallowed, flexing her tongue and cheeks around Tom, he shouted her name. His balls drew tight in her other hand. It might have been two decades since she'd made a man come, but she knew the warning signs pointed to Tom's impending explosion.

Willie hoped he wouldn't mind when she lifted off his steely erection as the first jet of semen shot from his balls. She wanted to watch. To see him unravel. The force of his orgasm was undeniable validation that she'd done a good job of pleasing her man.

Shocks of sympathy ecstasy lit up her nerve endings as she saw him shudder. He released a flood of come in a half dozen lines that slashed across his torso, nearly to his neck. All the while, she continued to pump, drawing more and more seed from him as he quaked and shouted in her hold.

When the blasts began to subside, she switched her grip so that her right hand still cupped his spent cock. Then she leaned to her left and sat up, her ass leaving her heels so she could observe the dazed bliss in his eyes, before laying her lips gently over his.

Tom kissed her endlessly as she brought him down from the impressive peak, eventually breaking the silky glides of their mouths to murmur repeated praise and thanks that inflated her self-confidence to roughly the size of the Partymobile bus the Hot Rods had built to take them all to Bare Natural for their destination weddings.

When he was able to open his eyes again and meet her stare, she relinquished her hold on his softening dick to rub the proof of his pleasure into his skin.

"Fuck, yes." He watched her fingers glide through the mess they'd made together. "See, nothing to it. Are you sure you aren't a pro?"

She smacked his belly then, making him grunt as satisfied laughter rang around them.

So it caught her off guard when he launched himself from the couch and tackled her to the floor, cradling her head so she landed softly in his sheltering arms. If she thought she'd tamed the beast in him, she'd been wrong. Knowing he'd allow her such liberty thrilled her. Witnessing the primal lust in his gaze as he studied her so intently made everything that had been dormant inside her roar to life.

"Tommy?" she whispered.

"Don't act shy and timid now." He growled against her neck

as he sucked hard, probably leaving a mark. "I've seen the real you, and I loved it. Give me that woman. Now."

Who was she to argue?

It felt so amazing to let the sensual side of her out after years of captivity.

This time when her mouth collided with Tom's, she met him for thrust after thrust of his tongue. Their teeth clicked together more than once. She didn't retreat, instead redoubling her efforts to consume him.

Tom grinned down at her for a moment then put his hands around her waist.

Before she realized what was happening, he'd lifted her, spun them, and flipped their positions. She sat on the couch with her thighs perched on his shoulders. He shoved the skirt of her sundress up then hummed as he buried his head between her legs and breathed deep, savoring the scent of her arousal.

He hauled her ass to the edge of the sofa then yanked her panties to the side before admiring the ladyscaping she'd done the night before. With a hum of approval, he fit his mouth to her pussy and began to drive her insane.

Pleasuring him had aroused her beyond belief and the deft flicks of his tongue over her clit, married with the prodding of his big fingers at the entrance of her body, made her sure that this was not going to be a prolonged experience.

Thank God.

Twenty-one years was long enough to wait for a spectacular orgasm at the hands of a man like him. Though, frankly, he was worth the wait. So was the ecstasy he began to deliver.

The tip of one finger penetrated her. It began to drill into her, working her open with short jabs that quickly became fluid glides as she soaked his hand with her natural lubrication. She shrieked, rubbing her fingers through his short hair as she pressed his face closer to her core.

He hummed against her, and then laughed a bit when she used her heels to press him tighter to her body. His hand skated up her ribs to her breast, squeezing it through her clothes as he devoured her.

A second finger joined the first, stretching her and filling her with awe as well as overwhelming rapture. When he curled them, stroking a place within her she hadn't known existed, she couldn't resist his delightful assault any longer.

"Tom!" She didn't even have the brainpower to tease him with his foolish nickname. "Yes. Please. Make me come."

He obliged with a swirl of his tongue around her clit and the bold pistoning of his digits within her.

Willie tensed, her entire body bent like a drawn bow. She hovered there, every cell in her body fully alive for the first time. Then she sprang apart, the tension released immediately when her climax erupted through her.

Tom never stopped. He groaned his encouragement against her swollen flesh as he continued to manipulate her body into giving up more and more pleasure to him. When finally she drooped, panting and limp against the cushions, she pried her eyes open to find him smiling at her, awfully smugly.

It took a few tries, but she finally managed to say softly, "Someone's confident in his performance."

"Damn straight." He licked his lips then grabbed his discarded shirt to wipe his glistening face. His scruff probably left some evidence of their experimentation behind on her thighs. She would wear the redness proudly.

Willie reached for his hand, so he entwined their fingers. "As you should be. That was…amazing."

Endorphins flooded her system, making her feel simultaneously relaxed and hyper-aware of everything pleasurable about this moment. Her body, singing. The warmth of their connection. The admiration in his gaze.

The unbelievably promising future she looked forward to for the first time in a while.

"Oh, honey. That wasn't the whole show. That was only a preview." He winked. "I haven't even gotten you naked yet. I can do a hell of a lot better than that."

"Tonight?" she whispered.

"Why waste any more time? I'm all about now." He scooted forward and scooped her into his arms. When he stood, carrying her toward the stairs, she gasped.

"Wait. I can't." Lightly, she pressed against his chest, getting his attention.

"What's wrong?" He frowned. "It *was* good, right?"

"It was everything," she answered honestly. "More than I expected, and definitely better than I remembered."

Did it make her disloyal to admit she might never have gone through her twenty-one-year dry spell if she knew sex could be that spectacular when gifted by a man who knew what he was doing?

"Then why?" He tipped his head to the side, studying her.

"Tom, I hate to break it to you, but I have an appointment in an hour." She cleared her throat. "If I had realized this was going to be an all-afternoon kind of session, I wouldn't have started it with you now. I'm sorry I didn't warn you earlier. I saw you and… Well, everything else flew out of my mind."

He grinned. "I can't be upset that you want me half as bad as I want you."

"So I should probably freshen up and head out if I'm going to make it to the doctor's office on time."

She hated the way he froze, his fingers clenching her thigh and ribs hard enough to leave bruises. Just like that, his lust evaporated, replaced by the terror she'd unintentionally triggered. "Everything all right?"

Oh, crap. She squirmed until he let her feet slide to the ground, though he still didn't relinquish his hold on her. Good thing, since her knees were still pretty wobbly.

His pulse hammered through the vein on his neck. She hugged him tight.

"Yes, of course. It's only a checkup, I swear. The doctor insists on it before she'll refill a prescription I have." Willie didn't want him to worry. Besides, she owed him complete disclosure if they were going to bind themselves more tightly together. "I thought I should start taking my anti-anxiety medicine again for a bit. The nightmares… And everything…"

Tom blinked a few times then nodded.

"I'm glad you're doing this if you think it will help." He slid his hands up until they rested on her back and he could tug her against his chest. "I'm sorry if I'm frightening you. I understand if *this* scares you, Willie. I admit, it's intense."

"You're not. It doesn't. Not after what we just did." She smiled then angled her face up to kiss his cheek. "It's a lot to handle at once, you know? Probably it'll be more, and faster even after today. Don't you think?"

Because now that she'd sampled the rapture he could bestow, there was no way she wanted to put on the brakes.

"I do." He nodded, still a little stiffer than usual. "Do you want me to drive you over there?"

In her younger years, she would have jumped on the offer.

"Thanks, but no. I've got this. It's no big deal." She kissed his cheek then peeked up at him through her lashes. "Why don't you stay here and come up with a way we can have the house to ourselves tonight?"

"I think that's the best idea you've ever had, Ms. Brown."

"Me too, Tommy." She winked at him then shrieked when he pinched her ass.

The slight sting and the resulting wash of pleasure inspired her to sprint up the stairs to the bathroom where she'd already stashed her toiletries, locking herself inside before they could get lost in each other again.

She'd never make it to her appointment if that happened.

⚡FIVE

Tom let go of the dead-man's switch on his lawn mower, letting the engine quit. He figured cutting the grass had to be preferable to pacing back and forth across his kitchen and living room, waiting for Willie to wrap up her doctor's visit and hit the grocery store. At least it accomplished something.

Hell, he should have insisted on going with her, not for her sake—though he'd gladly support her if she needed him to—but because he was half out of his mind with irrational terror.

Especially after she'd erased any lingering doubts about how compatible they were in bed as well as out of it.

He put the machine in the shed then plopped onto the floor of his front porch, his legs splayed and his heels propped halfway down the stairs as he chugged from the bottle of ice water he'd set out before beginning his manual labor distraction technique. Hand-in-hand-in-hand, Eli, his wife Sally, and his husband

Alanso came around the corner from the garage, heading for their apartment.

When they saw him, they detoured as if by tacit understanding.

Maybe someday Tom would have that kind of bond with Willie.

He pushed his sunglasses higher on his nose then plucked his shirt from the planks beside him, slinging it behind his neck so it draped over his shoulders, making room for one of the trio to sit down beside him. They worked hard. They'd be tired at the end of the day.

"Hey, Tom." Sally grinned as she jogged the last hundred feet to his perch while her husbands obviously enjoyed the view, staring at her ass.

"Hey, kid." He knocked his sweaty shoulder into hers.

"So…we saw Ms. Brown come over before. Did you fix things with her?" she asked.

"Think so." A grin threatened to crack his impartial façade.

"Then where's her car?" Alanso asked, rubbing his hand over his bald head.

"She's taking care of some stuff. Errands, appointments…" Tom couldn't bring himself to mention the doctor. He swallowed hard. "She should be back in an hour or two."

"Staying the night again, I hope?" Mustang Sally asked.

"Wow, you kids are terrible at subtlety." He shook his head.

"So level with us." Eli wrung his hands. "What's bugging you?"

"Nothing." He nearly choked on the lie, then deflected. "Look, I need to ask you a favor, and I don't want to hear any snide comments about it, either. Respect your elders for once.

Especially Willie. She's already kind of anxious about this whole thing between us. Don't make it worse."

"Got it." Alanso nodded. "How can we help? *Mierda*, you know we'd do anything for you two."

"It's Friday. Take Quinn over to the apartment. Order pizza, play some video games, and let him stay the night. He loves sleeping over there with you guys." Tom thought about it some more, then turned to Alanso. "In fact, maybe he can talk some more with you and Gavyn about Hot Rides. He's really into the motorcycles. Excited about them. You know how he hates to read?"

"Yeah, so." The Cuban guy shrugged. "I wasn't big into it either before I discovered titty mags."

Sally harrumphed.

Tom ignored them and went on. "Yesterday he asked if he could download a bunch of manuals and magazines to his tablet. He spent the whole night poring over them. It could be good for him to get more involved in the shop."

"No problem." Eli responded for them all though Alanso and Sally nodded, smiling. "But if you're going to have Ms. Brown alone tonight, you'd better hit the shower before she gets back."

"Planning on it. Who raised you to be such a smartass, anyway?" He whipped his shirt from around his neck and snapped it at his son, who easily dodged and laughed.

"Washing the stink off is a good start." Sally ignored their father-son antics and plowed ahead. "What else do you have up your sleeve?"

"I don't think we need the detailed plan of attack here, do we?" Alanso grimaced.

"No, no." She waved her hands in front of her chest. "I'm not asking what position he's going to do her in first, jeez. I meant, how are you going to woo her?"

"I'm a grown man. I don't *woo*." He snorted.

"Might want to rethink that, Dad." Eli suggested. "Especially your first time. Make it special. Play for keeps."

"Unlike your son, who forced me to check out a gay hookup spot before he saw the light. *Cabron*." Alanso crossed his arms, his thickening accent giving him away. He'd probably enjoyed that, at least a little.

Tom shook his head to keep from imagining it too clearly.

Maybe they had a point though. "I guess I could learn a thing or two from my kids. What do you suggest?"

Sally clapped. She grabbed his hands and tugged him toward the garden. "Start with flowers. She loves the pink ones."

By the time they'd gathered a bouquet and arranged it in a mason jar—since he apparently didn't own any vases anymore—Alanso had downloaded a romantic comedy from their streaming service. Eli had shoved the coffee table to one side of the living room and set out a blanket and put a bottle of white wine on ice in a bucket, instructing Tom to help Willie with dinner then take her on an indoor picnic. Mustang lit every candle he had in the house and scattered them around.

He felt kind of silly about the whole thing.

Until he surveyed their handiwork, looking at things from Willie's perspective. He could imagine her warm smile and her gratitude for anyone who paid special attention to her after so many years in the shadows. Then he realized his kids were kind of geniuses when it came to relationships. Had to be to pull off something like they had going on.

They were hanging out, getting ready to wrap things up and head back to their place, when banging on the door startled all of them.

It certainly wasn't Willie's dainty knock. Plus, Tom hoped she didn't bother with the formality anymore. He'd been pleased when she had come inside earlier, as if she belonged. Because she did. Only Bryce ever pounded that hard, when he was too lazy to use his own key or the one hidden under the mat.

Tom grouched, "It's open. Don't break the damn thing."

When Rick popped his head inside instead of one of the Hot Rods, Tom stood up straight, his slouch forgotten. This could not be good. "What are you doing back here so soon?"

"Why the hell aren't you answering your phone? I texted you about a dozen times in the past few hours," the investigator bitched as he strode into the kitchen.

"I've been...distracted." Okay, so really his phone had probably slipped out of the pocket of his jeans sometime after he'd tossed them on the floor. He hadn't noticed. *Shit.*

Rick stared at Tom for a few seconds then jerked his chin twice. First, toward the kids. Then again, toward the door.

"Eli, Sally, Al!" Tom barked. "Time to go. Quinn's probably starving. Get the kid his pizza, would you?"

"By now he's probably had Kaelyn cook him three gourmet dinners." Sally rolled her eyes.

"Pepperoni sounds good to me, *chica*." Alanso grinned. "Besides, Quinn could use some extra meals."

Mustang kissed Tom on the cheek and Alanso socked him on the shoulder. "Don't forget, you're the original Hot Rod. You've got this."

They went out the door together, arguing about toppings.

Eli was slower to follow. "Are you sure everything's okay, Dad?"

This time his nod came slower as he took in Rick's pinched face. "It will be. Go on."

"If you need—"

"Cobra. Now." His patience was running out as a million terrible thoughts barraged him at once.

"Okay, okay." Eli mumbled under his breath, something about *stubborn*.

Tom couldn't say he was wrong about that.

As Eli passed, Rick nodded, though his expression remained sober. As soon as the door clicked closed, he explained, "You know how I was going to start digging yesterday, in case I had to go deep into the archives to find any scraps of old news?"

"Yeah."

"Well, turns out it was a hell of a lot easier than I'd figured to get to the bottom of things." His fists balled, and he refused to meet Tom's gaze, staring at his shoes as if they were as fascinating as a naked woman. Never, in the years they'd known each other, had Rick had such a tough time sharing bad news.

"What the fuck is going on, Rick?" Tom widened his stance, readying himself for whatever was about to hit him.

No matter how prepared he thought he was, it didn't matter when he heard the report.

"It only took me a couple hours to uncover Steven Brown's social security number and shit like that I use in hunting information. And when I plugged it into my system, I did one better than scoring old articles or some junk. I found the man himself."

"What!" He nearly rocketed through the roof.

"He's alive, Tom."

His entire world shifted on its axis. In an instant he vacillated between disbelief, anger, shock, and panic. What would Willie say?

Never once did he doubt her account. "Willie really believes he's dead."

Tom didn't recognize the sound of his own voice.

"I know. Shit. Wait, it gets worse." Rick swallowed hard. When the big guy got nervous, Tom knew it was going to be horrific. "Not only is he alive, he doesn't live far away. Looks like he hopped the same bus line out of town Willie did. He's been living up in Delaware County for the past twenty or so years."

"That's only an hour from here." Tom clutched his chest, thankful he wasn't prone to heart attacks or he'd be having one right then. "What if they'd run into each other? That would have destroyed Willie."

He bent over, clutching his knees as he tried to suck in a couple solid lungfuls of air.

"Go ahead, take a minute. Get your shit together," Rick told Tom, his voice carefully modulated.

When Tom finally looked up, he had no idea how to proceed in reassembling the pieces of his plans for his future. And if he felt this way... Christ, what would this do to Willie? Would the news tear her apart?

No.

He would *not* let this slimy motherfucker hurt her again.

Tom punched the wall, making a hole in the sheetrock. He shook out his knuckles, not giving a fuck about the droplets of blood on them. Hell, how had Kaige survived so many similar punches? It was a miracle that kid could still use his fingers if it had hurt like that the million times he'd lost his cool.

"Hey, are you even listening to me?" Rick asked.

Tom had to shake his head to clear the rage.

"Go on." What else could there be to say?

"Keep your cool, swear it?" Rick pinched his nose between his thumb and forefinger.

"I think I'm a fucking saint at this point for shooting the shit here with you when I could be out searching for this asshole. Making sure he never messes with Willie again. Finding a permanent solution if I have to."

"You don't have to do that. Go looking for this dickhead, I mean." Rick drew in a deep breath. "I hope I'm not screwing this to hell, but that's why I was trying to call you earlier. I already picked the bastard up. He's sitting out back right now. I went asking questions and he kind of put two and two together. I thought it was safer if I brought him, kept an eye on him, rather than letting him roam around on his own after that. He came with me because he wants to see Willie again."

Tom's head verged on exploding. He'd never been so furious in his life, except maybe at the universe in general when it had stolen his wife. This time he had a target for that ferocious hostility.

He whipped around and stormed down the short hallway, past the half bath, then wrenched open the back door so hard he popped one of the hinges off. Sure enough, some dude huddled on the bench beside it, looking like he was about to shit his pants when he caught a glimpse of Tom's once-in-a-lifetime-level wrath, aimed squarely in his direction.

Steven motherfucking Brown.

He wasn't as dumb as he might seem. He took one look at Tom and started to run.

Not nearly fast enough.

Tom snatched the bastard by his collar, whipped him around, then planted his already aching fist in the guy's face. Steven's head snapped back and he crashed to the porch. That only made more work for Tom, who hauled the guy up with his mostly numb right hand then hit him again, with his fresh left.

While the guy was writhing on the ground, Tom fought off Rick's restraining hands to land a kick to the asshole's ribs that sent him tumbling down the stairs and into the grass below. He would have kept going, past all sense and ethics if it hadn't been for his kids, who never listened worth a damn.

Eli charged around the corner of the house with Kaige and Roman a couple steps behind. "Dad! What the fuck?"

It said something that the guys first made sure the man on the ground wasn't going anywhere before they looked to Tom for direction.

"Who the hell is this?" Roman asked, unconcerned about the gash on the dude's face or the ones on Tom's hands. Barracuda was an infamous fighter himself, nothing here he hadn't seen before.

"Not for you to worry about," Tom barked at the same time the dumb fuck on the ground tried to speak around a cough.

"Steven—Help me."

Begging for mercy wouldn't do him any good. Not in Tom's book. He reared up again, ready to swing. Kaige grabbed him in a bear hug and forced him back. "This isn't you. Calm down. You're freaking me out, Tom. In all the years that I struggled with my temper, I've never once seen you lose yours. Come on.

Don't make a liar out of yourself. You told me violence isn't the answer. Did you mean that?"

He had. Until today.

"Settle down, Tom." Rick joined Kaige while Eli and Roman stood guard over their visitor. "We've got to talk to him. Find out his story. We can't do that if you knock his ass out."

Tom swallowed his fury. It took a couple minutes, but eventually the haze cleared enough that he could read the confusion and fear in his sons' faces. Even Roman was rubbing his hand on his coveralls repeatedly, about as expressive as he got.

He held his hands up, palms out, wincing at the sting in his fingers. "You're right. I'm better now. Sorry."

Steven acted like that apology had been aimed in his direction.

Rick nudged him with the toe of his shoe. "Keep quiet, we're trying to save your hide. Though I'm not sure you deserve it."

"What can we do?" Eli asked.

"Go home," Tom said.

"I shouldn't have left the first time!" His son threw his arms wide, palms up in disbelief. "Now you want me to do it again?"

"I'm here," Rick reminded them. "I think your dad's right. We need to talk to Steven alone before anyone else is involved. If things get out of control, I'll call you. I promise."

"And when this guy leaves, you'll let me know everything is okay?" Eli asked Tom.

"Yeah. I can do that." Though nothing would be all right. How could it be?

The three Hot Rods looked at each other, then backed away, toward their apartment.

"Kaige! Not one *single* word of this to your wife." Tom didn't flinch from Nova's questioning stare. Nor did he dare to drop Nola's distinct name in front of her father. "Actually, not to anyone. This stays between us."

"We don't keep secrets from each other, you know that." Roman leapt to Kaige's defense.

"This one time. It's absolutely necessary." Tom's tone brooked no argument.

"Did Rick call that dude Steven?" Kaige asked Eli.

Cobra nodded slightly and Kaige turned an unhealthy shade of purple. He knew.

Eli cursed a streak. Roman, too. They must have figured it out, though Tom wasn't sure how except those kids seemed to share one mind.

"This is not your fight. Go home. And say *nothing*," Tom ordered.

Nova, Eli, and Roman looked hurt that Tom banished them. That betrayal was nothing compared to what Nola would feel if she knew her dad was right out back of her apartment, where she cradled this undeserving fuck's grandbaby. Tom refused to allow the creep to realize how close his family was in case he decided to cause trouble for them.

It was a lie for the greater good. Necessary.

"Swear it. On Hot Rods."

"Yeah. I swear." Kaige nodded then spit in the direction of the guy in Tom and Rick's clutches.

"Tomorrow, you're going to come clean." Eli glared at Tom, then at Willie's dead-but-not-so-dead husband. "Hiding the truth has hurt enough people already. Don't you do it too, Dad."

Tom nodded, message received though he had no idea if he

could live up to his son's standards. With them gone, he turned to Rick. "Bring him in, will you?"

"Sure."

Steven groaned as Rick hauled him to his feet then steered him toward the busted door and into Tom's sanctuary. As he took in the candles, flowers, and foolish date-night accessories lying around, Tom realized this couldn't happen here.

Not now.

Willie could come home any second.

"Actually, we need to get out of here," Tom told Rick. "Can we take this to your office instead?"

"Of course. I was going to suggest the same thing."

Tom rushed outside once more, terrified they'd meet Willie in the parking lot. He didn't even bother to blow out the candles before they left.

It was a tense ride into the heart of Newburgh, the nearest decent-sized city to Middletown, where Rick had a commercial space in a four-story building. They'd never done business here before, preferring to speak in the comfort of Tom's home. He was impressed by the well-lit, modern space. "Huh."

"What'd you expect? Some dump in a basement filled with cigarette smoke and bad sleuth novels?" Rick grunted as he shoved Steven out of the elevator and into a modest conference room.

Tom might have laughed if his entire existence wasn't hanging in the balance of this solitary conversation.

"Okay, we're here. Now spill." Rick took charge, grilling Mr. Brown. "Tell us what happened the night you supposedly died or we'll call the cops and have you arrested for fraud and anything else I can think of between now and when they arrive."

Steven sighed. "Honestly, I don't mind. It feels good to finally get it off my chest."

"This isn't some kind of confessional," Tom snarled. He certainly wasn't about to absolve the man of his sins.

Rick shook his head at Tom and he bit his tongue. Hard.

"Why're you so bent out of shape, anyway, huh?" Steven leaned forward. "Do you know Wilhelmina? You got a thing for my wife? Is that why you came all the way up north to track me down?"

"Willie is *not* yours," Tom snarled, nearly abandoning the shred of self-control Kaige had helped him recover. "Hasn't been since you disappeared on her. What happened that night? What'd you do, survive the wreck and have amnesia for twenty-one fucking years? You sick fuck! Did you move up here to spy on her? To gloat at her pain, knowing she mourned you when you'd simply abandoned her? How fucking dare you even look at her?"

Steven seemed dazed by the volley of antagonistic questions. "I don't even know what to say to that. Do you mean Wilhelmina lives near here? I… No, I had no idea."

Rick intervened, steering them in the right direction. "Why don't you start with the accident. Tell us what happened."

"I faked it. All of it." Steven put his head in his hands, which was when Tom noticed that they were shaking. Violently. "I didn't know what the hell else to do."

"What do you mean?" Rick asked in a kinder tone. Was he playing good cop, or did he actually feel bad for this dirtwad? He sank into one of the chairs at the head of the table. Though it wasn't what he wanted, Tom lowered himself into one across the way from Steven, hoping they'd get more out of the man if they weren't so adversarial.

Besides, as much as he hated to admit it, something about Steven was starting to make him feel kind of bad. With his chin lowered to his chest, he slumped there, unfolding his hands on the table limply, palms up. He clearly wasn't happy about the situation.

His chin trembled as he looked at Rick. "People were threatening Willie and my kids. They didn't approve of me marrying a black woman, never mind 'breeding' with her, as they put it. I was young and scared for them. Myself, too."

He sighed.

They waited for him to elaborate.

"It got so bad that I started finding dead animals around. Small stuff at first…one of those dark-brown mice, then a crow in my locker at work. A black and white spotted rabbit, stuffed into our mailbox. I hardly had time to slam the door closed on that one before my daughter Amber saw it with its eyeballs hanging out. Then a week later, someone skinned a black cat, glued its pelt to my windshield with its own blood then smeared the guts and bones and shit all over my car. I had to stop and wash it before I could go home." He shook his head. "There were letters too, warnings. Saying next they'd go after my daughters. Do worse even to them. Called them an abomination when they were the best thing in my life."

This time he broke, sobbing as he remembered the horrors he'd been subjected to.

"Why wasn't there any record of this with the police?" Tom

asked, since that's the first place he'd looked. Scouring public files was one of the things he'd learned from Rick.

"They said not to tell." Steven shrugged one shoulder. "What was I supposed to do?"

"Pack up your family and get the hell out of there!" Tom glared, though he realized it was easy to judge in hindsight.

"We didn't have the money for that." He groaned. "Hell, there were times I had to pawn things to put food on the table, not that I told Wilhelmina. I was embarrassed that I wasn't better for her. That I couldn't do anything about the trouble we were in or making a better life for us. It got so bad… I figured, they'd be better off without me."

Rick cursed.

"So that they could fend for themselves against these ignorant assholes?" Tom tried not to shout.

"The way I saw it, if I was dead, they'd get our insurance money and my pension from my job. It wasn't a lot, but it would be enough to move on. So I stole a vehicle out of a lot near work after everyone else had finished our shift, I snuck back to the factory and broke the lock. Used the equipment there to weld the bumpers of the two cars together, front to back. Who knew that shit job would come in handy one day? I drove the cars a little ways down the street to the bridge, and waited. When I saw those lights coming, I used the stolen car to push ours. I didn't know if it would work at all, but damn, when it crashed into the side of that delivery truck, ripped the bumper right off the car I'd stolen, then flipped over the bridge, I knew I couldn't go back. I took off right that minute. Drove myself straight to the bus terminal and hopped on the first one out of town."

"You never bothered to check in on your family, to make sure they were all right when you left them undefended?" Tom felt his anger building again.

"I couldn't risk it." Steven put his face in his hands.

"Because let me tell you, after you *died*, Willie fell apart. Grief-stricken, terrified, and broke, she had nothing but her own smarts and determination on her side. Hell, for a while there, her and the girls were homeless. Anything could have happened to them."

"What?" Steven's head snapped up.

Rick nodded, his features locked in a grave expression. "There was no money. I checked. Not from insurance, because they ruled it a possible suicide. And not from the company, because they said you didn't have enough service time in. Looks like they were paying your overtime off the books so the credits didn't count."

"No! That can't be true!" Steven struggled to rise then. Rick kept him in place with a firm hand on his shoulder.

"It is. My wife died. You have no idea what I would have given to still have her by my side. I'd do anything to make it work. And you threw yours away." Tom couldn't possibly think less of this coward. Or maybe he could. "For that matter, you left your kids to survive, sometimes on the streets. How could you do that to your own flesh and blood?"

Rick reached over from where he sat between the two men in his office to splay his hand on Tom's chest, just in case he got any more urges to resort to violence.

Tom had heard enough. All he could stand for one evening. "Will you keep an eye on him? Don't let him disappear."

"Sure, of course." Rick nodded. "When we finish up here, I'll drive Steven home. It's the weekend. You don't have to be at work until Monday, right?"

The guy nodded, looking like he might drown in his own misery before then.

"You're going to stay in your house. No phone calls either." Tom leaned across the table to get up in his face. "I need some time to make this right. There's no way I can fix your mistakes, but I'm hoping to God I can keep them from causing any more damage than they already have."

Steven nodded again. "Do whatever you can for Wilhelmina, please."

For a moment, Tom pitied the bastard.

What a mess.

"You need a ride?" Rick asked.

"Nah. I'll call a cab." He scrubbed his face. "I owe you for this."

"It's not what I hoped we'd find."

"I know, none of us did." Tom swallowed hard then left the office, shutting the door so quietly, it should have scared them more than if he'd slammed the thing. What the fuck was he going to do now?

Tell Willie the truth and shatter the world she'd rebuilt for herself?

Keep it from her and try to advance their relationship with some horrible secret wedged between them?

Fuck, there was no way he could sleep with her tonight, knowing this. It wouldn't be right. Unlike Steven, Tom didn't believe in taking the easy way out.

Willie deserved better than that.

He wanted nothing less than to be the person who wounded her, but he couldn't see any way around it either. He needed time to think about how to handle this best.

Why? Why did shit like this have to happen to them? Weren't they decent? Didn't they deserve better?

Fuck. He hadn't resorted to self-pity in years.

It just felt as if he'd been so damn close to claiming something amazing and rare.

Tom smacked his hand on a light post as he approached the street, wincing as the impact split open his knuckles again. The superficial wounds were nothing compared to the damage he was about to inflict on the woman he had come to love.

Fuck his life.

≋SIX

Willie sang along with the radio as she drove into town. She arrived at the medical complex a couple minutes early, as usual. That gave her plenty of time to stop by the lab on her way in and have her blood drawn for the standard tests the doctor would order as a precaution.

Needles didn't bother her. A quick pinch, some chatting with the cute young phlebotomist—whose nametag declared her Casey Lu—and she was on her way down the hallway to her doctor's suite with some gummy candy the woman had shared from her stash to sweeten the deal.

Serene music drifted through the waiting room as she checked in at the front desk then skimmed the home decorating magazines. She wondered how Tom would feel about them giving his place a facelift. Would it be too presumptuous to suggest? Or would he welcome the change as they made his place *their* place?

Her toe tapped on the industrial carpeting as she grew impatient.

He was waiting for her.

Tonight was going to be their night.

Finally.

"Wilhelmina Brown?" The nurse opened the door to the patient rooms and called her inside. The woman ushered her toward the full scale. For the first time in years, Willie worried about what it would say. It'd been a while since she'd bothered to really watch her figure, though she tended to have a pretty decent metabolism. There'd been so many times when she'd been on a diet—enforced by her lack of cash, to ensure her kids had as much as she could give them to eat—that when things had finally picked up with her sewing clients and they got back on their feet, she'd splurged.

She never bought anything but whole milk or real butter. And she baked often.

Tom hadn't seemed to have any complaints, though he'd yet to see her entirely nude.

Willie decided that was all that mattered to her. She averted her gaze while the woman pushed weights up and down the horizontal bar then nodded as she noted the number in her file. Willie didn't bother to look. She liked herself just fine no matter what.

After ushering her into a patient room, the nurse asked a bunch of questions about how she'd been feeling lately.

"Not terrible." Willie shrugged. "There's been a lot of stress. My younger daughter got married, had a baby, and her sister met a great man, who's had some problems with drinking and drugs. Combined, that caused a lot of drama and I think it's getting to me a bit. Headaches now and then, and a bunch of nightmares."

"That sounds reasonable given the situation. I'll make a note and you can discuss it with the doctor." The lady smiled then talked some about her own kids and their antics. As they chatted, she took Willie's blood pressure.

When the nurse went to add the data to Willie's chart, she hummed then double-checked the readout on the wall.

"Something wrong?" Willie wondered.

"Not exactly. It's in the normal range. Higher than your average though."

"Figures." She laughed. Getting her hands on Tom London would probably always have that effect on her. "I sort of met a guy. He's my new son-in-law's father. And we were…you know…not too long before I came here."

"Way to go." The nurse winked. "I'd say that's a pretty great reason for the difference. Good for the heart, too."

In more ways than one, Willie thought.

Her giant smile must have given her away.

"Well, congratulations." The nurse gathered up her things. "Dr. Smith should be in shortly. Enjoy the rest of your day."

"I will." She tried not to purr at the thought of what awaited her at home.

It wasn't much longer before her physician entered and they said their hellos while the woman reviewed the notes in her file. "So, tell me more about these headaches you've been having."

"Pretty much the same as I've had periodically in the past. A throbbing at the base of my skull. Like the tension headaches you've treated me for before. I just haven't needed my medicine for those, or the anxiety pills, in a while so everything is expired."

"Any flashing lights or dizziness?"

"I've felt lightheaded a couple times lately. It passes quickly." She shrugged. "A few weeks ago I had a fuzzy spot in my right eye. I know you probably hate to hear this, but I looked it up online and it matched depictions of an ocular migraine. Twinkling, a sort of prism effect, bright. It only lasted a half hour or so before it faded. I was nervous at first, never saw so many fun colors before. Didn't hurt though, and like I said, it faded pretty quickly."

Dr. Smith smiled softly. "This one time, I'll say you probably got that right. As long as you're not driving when it hits, they're usually not an issue. Let me take a quick look at a few things and I think we'll have you on your way."

She peeked in Willie's ears, listened to her heart and breathing then paused as she looked up.

"Another deep breath?" Willie asked.

"No, sorry. It's just that your pupils are slightly different sizes." Dr. Smith walked over to her file and flipped some pages, then clicked through the laptop that held older records. "Hmm… I've never noticed anisocoria on you before. Do you have a little more time this afternoon?"

"I'm free, yes." Willie bit her lip.

"I'm going to write an order for a scan at the imaging center downstairs. I think it wouldn't hurt to be safe. You're not afraid of cramped quarters, are you? I can have them start your anti-anxiety medicine as well. If you need something faster acting, they can crush some Valium and put it under your tongue." Dr. Smith was already scribbling something on a pad she drew from her coat pocket.

Willie thought back to the era she'd spent living in the van.

That would have been impossible if she was claustrophobic. "I'll be fine."

"Okay, then." Dr. Smith smiled, though it seemed slightly more forced than before. "I checked you in from my laptop here. Head down to the first floor. Go to the end of the hall and you'll see a waiting room on the left. Shouldn't take more than an hour, probably less."

"Thank you." She hopped off the table and gathered her belongings then wandered through the medical center, trying not to imagine the time Tom, Eli, and Michelle had spent in facilities like these.

When she arrived at the imaging office, a young man was waiting for her. He led her straight into the back, had her lie on a table and close her eyes as the open-air machine worked its magic. She used the time to daydream about the things she wanted to try with Tom later that night.

The tech told her he was finished and she prepared to leave. Curious, she asked, "So what happens now?"

"We'll have a specialist read the scans and send Dr. Smith a report. Most likely they'll send you a letter letting you know everything's cool." He grinned. "If something turns up, they'll give you a call. So don't panic if you don't hear anything right away. Most people hate the waiting. That's actually good news."

"Okay, great. Thank you." She glanced at her watch, eager to finish up her shopping then get back to Hot Rods. It was already later than their usual suppertime and she wanted to whip up something special for Tom. Maybe crab cakes or duck breast with raspberry sauce. He'd loved both when she'd made them in the past.

She didn't mind admitting to herself that she'd been trying to impress him with her cooking. Looks like it had worked.

Willie drove her cart through the grocery store aisles so fast she ended up taking one of the corners on two wheels. Grinning, she thought she deserved to be an honorary Hot Rod.

So when she pulled into the lot at the garage, she was surprised that Tom didn't come out to help carry in the groceries like he usually did. The bays at Hot Rods were closed, early for the kids to call it a night. With a shrug, she hefted as many bags as she possibly could—only suckers made more trips than necessary—then headed for the house.

Her load banged into the door as she reached for the knob. It surprised her when it swung inward. "Tommy? Could you give me a hand with the groceries, please?"

No response.

He never left the door unlocked when he was out, and certainly not standing open. Even though Middletown wasn't especially high in crime, he didn't tempt fate considering the constant flow of cars at the gas station out front.

What was going on?

When she pushed into the kitchen, she gasped.

Was this some kind of setup? There were flowers on the kitchen table and lovely candlelight danced around the room. She smiled and got misty eyed when she peeked into the living room and saw the blanket and wine he'd spread out for them plus more of the same there, too.

He must have run over to the apartment quickly for something.

She might as well get started on dinner since he'd gone to a lot of trouble to make their night special. Adding a few touches of her own seemed only fair.

Singing to herself, she danced her way around the kitchen from the refrigerator to the stove as she gathered ingredients and began to mix the crab cakes she'd decided on. When she had the patties formed, she popped them back into the refrigerator and set some water to heat up for the pasta she'd make to accompany them. In the meantime, she apologized mentally to Dr. Smith then used some heavy cream as a base for a sage-lime sauce.

When she had all that finished, she glanced at the clock, frowning.

She scrubbed her hands, then took her phone from her purse. No messages.

With a swipe of her finger, she tapped out a note to Tom. *Dinner should be ready in twenty minutes.*

Then she combined some pudding and whipped cream. Chocolate pie wasn't her fanciest dessert ever. It was quick and easy to prepare, though. Plus, it could be used in about a million different creative and naughty ways.

Her phone beeped. She practically knocked half her ingredients onto the floor when she lunged for it.

Sorry, Willie. Something came up. Not sure how long I'll be. Go ahead without me if you're hungry.

Was the man nuts? She wasn't about to spoil this. Of course she would wait for him.

In fact, she decided she might as well make one of his fantasies come true. So she shucked her dress and underwear, then grabbed the apron she'd brought over and left on the hook on the back of the pantry door. She put it on, feeling kind of ridiculous.

Tom's expression would be worth it.

Maybe they wouldn't be eating until much later.

Of course, after an hour had gone by, she was curled up on the blanket in front of the TV, partway through the movie she'd found ready and waiting. Her ass had gone numb a while ago from sitting on the floor and she'd wrapped herself in an afghan that normally decorated the back of the couch, since her apron didn't provide much warmth.

She clutched her phone, checking every minute or two for an update from Tom. Nothing.

Sickness roiled in her guts as she tried not to associate tonight's foiled special meal with the last one she'd prepared for a man.

Or maybe that was hunger?

When the credits on the movie rolled, she could no longer deny her growling stomach.

Part annoyed and part scared, she hustled into the kitchen and fried the crab cakes, smacking the pan on the burner harder than she otherwise would. Half the water in the pot had disappeared. She didn't bother to replace it, instead making less pasta. Her cream sauce had a skin on top of it that only ticked her off more.

Still, she carefully prepared two plates then wrapped one in aluminum foil and popped it into the stove, which she left on warm. She blew out the nearly spent candles in the kitchen on her way back to the living room. At the last second, she paused then backed up.

Where had that hole in the wall come from?

She ran her fingers over the crater, wondering if Quinn had been playing basketball in the house again. He'd have to use his next video chat with the Powertools crew to learn how to patch drywall since she was sure Tom would hold him accountable for the damage. *No time like the present to learn new skills, kid.*

A few hours with her absent and things went to hell.

Normally, she might have chuckled at her dramatics. Tonight, she sat in the living room, eating her food without enjoying it much. Only a couple candles flickered near her now, so it was nearly as dark in the room as it was in her thoughts.

A light throbbing began in her temples. Great.

Setting her dish aside on the coffee table, she rested her eyes, hoping to relax enough that the pain subsided on its own. Sure, she had the prescriptions she'd gotten filled while she shopped, but she preferred not to take the medicine unless she really needed it.

Sometime later, a key sliding into the lock startled her awake.

Though she was a little annoyed and a lot worried, she couldn't help but smile when Tom came through the door. "Hey."

"Oh, Willie." He grimaced. "Shit. I ruined our plans. I'm sorry."

"It's okay. Must have been important." Curiosity was about to rip her apart.

"Yeah. Someone I wasn't expecting came into town…" He wouldn't look at her when he said, "They had some news for me that I didn't want to hear and I don't really know what to do about it yet."

The absolute misery in his gaze nearly eviscerated her. Comforting him was the only thing she could think about.

"Then why don't we forget it for tonight." She smiled softly.

He'd tell her when he was ready. "I left some crab cakes and pasta warming for you. There's even chocolate pie."

His Adam's apple bobbed hard a few times, as if he were swallowing back bile. Not exactly the reaction she'd hoped for. When he unlaced his boots, kicked them off onto the mat by the door, then headed for the stove, she expected him to collect his reward.

Instead, he took the plate out and put it in the refrigerator.

A part of her wanted to cry for the wasted effort. Had she judged him so wrong?

She looked around, wishing she could reach her dress without exposing her nakedness. If she could, she'd put it on and make a run for it. Something had gone off track here.

"Sorry, Willie. It's kind of late for rich food. I'm not very hungry right now either." He approached her slowly, as if unsure of what to say or do. Was he going to leave her there?

Tom sighed, then sank down beside her. He reached out as if he was going to touch her cheek with his fingertips.

And that's when she noticed how torn up his knuckles were.

"Tommy!" she gasped. "What happened to your poor hands?"

He didn't answer right away, staring down at them as he flexed his fingers slowly while wincing.

"Wait, is *this* what made that hole in the kitchen wall? Did *you* put it there?" Her eyes widened. He never lost his temper.

"Something like that." Again, he dodged.

When she climbed to her knees to peer at him eye to eye, as if she could read whatever was troubling him better that way, the afghan slipped from around her.

Tom groaned. He muttered something she couldn't quite

make out. It sounded an awful lot like *gonna murder that bastard for making me miss out* though.

So she did the only thing she knew how to do. She offered herself as his remedy for whatever had gone wrong.

Willie collected every bit of nerve she had, then took the blanket off her entirely. She smiled at Tom then walked the apron up her thighs. Higher and higher, she raised the hem until she whipped it over her head and knelt before him entirely nude.

A growl left his throat a moment before he eliminated the gap between them and fused their mouths together. His kiss held a note of desperation she'd never noticed before. It reminded her of the way she'd felt when he hadn't come home. Scared shitless. He crushed their lips together and ravaged her until she moaned, needing more.

Frantically, she reached for him, hoping to tear his clothes off.

Her hands slid beneath his shirt then skimmed up his back, letting her nails scratch lightly along either side of his spine as she drew them down again, then around his waist.

But as her hand cupped his crotch, she felt he wasn't even hard for her.

When she froze, he must have realized something was wrong.

"Sorry, Willie." He put some space between them, then mumbled, "I want to, but I don't think I can. Guess my age is showing. Earlier today. God. That was amazing. I'm not a young stud anymore."

"Maybe not, but you're all the man I can handle." She hugged him and thought she felt him shy away from her hold. Why? "You would tell me if I did something to upset you, right?"

He cursed then rubbed his eyes. "You're not the problem here, Willie."

"Is it the doctor visit that's still bothering you?" Hating to bring it up, she winced.

"Ah, shit. I forgot about that."

He had? She found that hard to believe, given his earlier freak-out.

Tom sighed, getting his breathing under control. He leaned over and grabbed some pillows from the couch then tossed them onto the floor. With a few efficient movements, he got rid of his shirt and pants then sprawled on his back in his briefs. The sight of him like that did nothing to calm her rioting hormones.

Until he patted the spot next to him on their picnic quilt.

"Come here and let me hold you?" he asked.

Willie definitely wasn't going to turn down that offer when everything inside her was jumbled and in need of reassurance. She snuggled beside him, draping her arm over his middle and resting her head on his chest. The feel of so much of her skin pressed to his for the first time was nearly as pleasurable as when he'd gone down on her before.

Almost.

"Everything go okay at your appointment?" he wondered as he stroked her hair, making the escalating thump of her headache seem less drastic. Whatever had gone wrong, they could work through it if they kept talking. Communication was typically one of their strengths.

"Pretty much." She lifted one shoulder where he trailed his fingers across the chilled skin. "Got my prescriptions and they did some precautionary testing."

"Have you taken your medicine yet?" he asked. "I know you don't like to rely on it. If you went through the effort of going to get it, I'm guessing you really need it."

She squashed the urge to massage her own scalp.

"I'll take that as a no. Where is it? I'll get it for you." He set her aside and got to his feet then followed her instructions to her purse. When he returned with a giant glass of water and the pills, she accepted them.

Then they resumed their positions, lying together in silence for a while.

Willie hated to destroy their temporary truce. A splinter of worry kept stabbing at her though and she figured it was better to express it than let it fester.

"Whatever happened today hurt you. I understand if you need time to process it. But I don't like being kept in the dark. Not when I might be able to help you otherwise." She tried not to get upset. At Tom, or herself, or whatever was eating him.

It was difficult when disappointment, fear, and longing tangled together into a knot in her belly. He'd always been open and honest with her in their lengthy conversations. Even when discussing difficult topics.

Having him change that now, when they were supposed to be drawing closer instead of falling further apart, bruised her heart. It felt as if he was eroding part of the foundation they'd built their relationship on.

His mouth opened then closed a few times, like he might respond. Or say something. Anything.

In the end, he simply kissed her forehead and held her tighter.

When her medicines began to kick in and her eyelids grew heavy, Willie dragged the afghan over them and blew out the lone remaining candle.

In the pitch blackness, she whispered, "Good night, Tommy."

It nearly broke her heart when his ragged voice murmured back, "I love you, Willie. No matter what, please never forget that."

She would have said it back if she hadn't been so shocked, or if he hadn't put his fingers over her lips to keep her from having to reply.

"Go to sleep, honey." The rapid rise and fall of his chest as he sighed, lifted then dropped her, too. Just like the events of the day had done. "I really am sorrier than you know."

Since he wouldn't let her speak, and she wasn't sure she had the right answers anyway in the midst of her confusion, she closed her eyes and let the chemicals she'd ingested—and the warm strength of Tom's arms around her—assist her in drifting off.

SEVEN

Tom couldn't believe it when sunlight began to trickle through the curtains, dusting Willie's face with the first golden beams of morning. He hadn't slept at all, instead spending hours memorizing the curve of her nose and the way her thick lashes rested on her bold cheekbones in case this was the last time he got the privilege of holding her through the night.

He'd thought of every possible move he could make and what the resulting outcomes might be. The bitch of it was, he still had no idea how to break the news to Willie in the least hurtful way, though he couldn't imagine doing anything else.

Ironically, she hadn't had her nightmare.

Either the medicine had worked, she'd exhausted herself worrying about him and his absurd behavior, or—some paranoid part of him worried—maybe subconsciously she could tell what he'd been hiding.

The really fucked-up part of it all was that when he should be focused only on her, he kept fighting selfishness. Would she stay with him, knowing her beloved Steven was still out there and available? Hell, even through Tom's anger, it had been obvious the man worshipped *Wilhelmina*.

Tom couldn't fault him for that.

She was spectacular—a fighter disguised in pretty dresses behind soft words.

Nor would he blame her if she wanted another try at life with her husband by her side, though he still believed she deserved better than someone who would cut and run, no matter the circumstances.

The more he looked at her, his chest aching at the thought of losing her now that he'd only finally seemed to have a shot at a future with her, the more he realized how epically dumb he'd been wasting time this past year. If he'd acted sooner on the admiration, lust, and respect he felt for her, maybe they'd be solid enough that even Steven Brown wouldn't have a shot at tearing them apart.

Tom placed a light kiss on her forehead, ridiculously pleased when she smiled and burrowed into his chest in her sleep. Then he carefully untangled himself from her and stood. For a few more minutes, he watched her, terrified to leave.

Then he quietly backed up the first couple stairs before turning and heading to his room. He hauled out fresh clothes, tugging on jeans and holding his shirt in his hands as he stared into the mirror.

The chain with his wedding ring glinted in the soft light. He lifted the gold to his lips, kissed it, then reached behind him to unclasp the chain for the first time in thirteen years.

Willie had been as understanding as always of his souvenir from a brilliant past. That didn't mean she should have to share his future with ghosts. *If* she cared to spend any of it with him. And that was a big fucking if at this point.

He crossed to the hand-carved wooden box he'd made for other mementos, like the newspaper article Willie had mentioned, then lifted the lid. Safely tucking the necklace inside, he shut it once more, his hand lingering over it while he caught his breath.

"See you on the other side," he whispered, then yanked his shirt over his head.

Tom jogged down the stairs as quietly as possible and let himself out. When he hit the ground, he ran faster. Over to the open-backed metal staircase that led to the second-story Hot Rods apartment. He took the stairs two at a time, but didn't stop when he got to the landing, instead continuing around the bend and up to the rooftop deck his kids had built for sunning themselves, enjoying the view of the fields that stretched beyond Middletown, barbequing and doing who-knew-what together out of sight from the rest of the world below.

He plopped onto one of the lounge chairs and hauled out his phone to text Eli.

Meet me upstairs. Bring Nova.

He figured there'd be no keeping Kaige away since his wife was every bit as snarled in this mess as Willie.

Rebel, too. Bryce was the largest, most intimidating of the bunch, even though Roman was far deadlier in a fight.

Tom hoped it didn't come to action again. He hated that

he'd given in to base instincts the day before. As he sat there, he heard the familiar engine of Willie's car as it started then began to fade. He jogged to the side of the garage's roof deck in time to see her taillights zipping away. *Shit!*

Crushing every impulse that screamed at him to chase her down and bring her back, to explain why he'd acted like such a moron the night before, he made sure he did things right. If that meant letting her stew at her house for a couple of hours until he could slice her with the accuracy of a surgeon's scalpel instead of blasting her full-force, resulting in the traumatic mess a shotgun would inflict, he'd do that.

He stared at the sky, trying not to give in to the urge to pummel the concrete wall beneath his fists. Slowly, he stepped away from the edge and sank into a chair again.

Before long, boots clomped up the metal stairs. Then three of his sons joined him, spreading out in a semi-circle around where he sat. They stood, arms crossed and feet spread, looking every bit the badasses they could have become if he hadn't rescued them from hard-knock lives on the streets.

"It was really him, wasn't it?" Kaige didn't bother with hellos. "Nola's dad?"

Tom nodded, wincing. "You didn't say anything, did you? I haven't told Willie yet."

"Fuck," Eli snarled.

"Hang on a minute." Bryce's stare whipped between them all. "Are you saying the guy isn't dead?"

"Pretty sure it wasn't a phantom's nose that did this to my hand." Tom held up his fingers for inspection.

"Ho-ly fuck." The big guy wavered for a moment. "How did this happen?"

Tom explained everything. How he'd asked Rick to help find closure for Willie and had inadvertently opened a much bigger can of worms, dumb shit that he was. Still, he'd rather have her find out like this than because she ran into the guy out in public somewhere at random. Worse, Steven could have eventually wised up and come after her, or tried to use his marriage to her for some underhanded purpose, like stealing her social security or some shit later on.

A man who lied about dying might be unethical and dangerous in any number of ways.

"She knows something's up. I didn't come home until late last night. Blew our date to hell." He scrubbed his hands over his face. At the moment he didn't care if he was about to drop too much information on his kids. It was payback for the zillions of times they'd done it to him, either because they legitimately needed advice about a personal situation or because they liked to bust his balls. "I couldn't get it up knowing I was lying to her. It didn't feel right to make love to her under those circumstances."

"Ugh!" Eli looked away.

Bryce frowned then nodded.

"I can see that." Rebel put his huge hand on Tom's shoulder. "I think you made the right call there."

"We can't keep this a secret," Kaige jumped in, worry for his wife and daughter evident in the deep lines scoring his face. "This guy knows where they are now. Or he'll figure it out soon enough. We have to get it on the table before someone gets hurt. Son of a bitch...*more* hurt."

"That's why I'm here," Tom agreed. "We're gonna take Willie, Nola, and Amber over there to confront Steven. They have a right to know the truth and decide what to do with that information. We're also going to have their backs. They're not going in alone."

"We'll leave the rest of the guys here to watch over Ambrose and Quinn. They don't belong in the middle of this." Eli made Tom proud with his total understanding. Maybe he'd done something right in his life, raising these kids.

"Exactly."

"When are we leaving?" Kaige asked.

"Why don't you round up Nola and Amber. Gavyn, too," Tom instructed, forming a plan. "I'll go get Willie. I think I should tell her alone. When she's ready, I'll text you to bring the girls over so she can share with them, if she decides that's what's best. I don't know that there's much we can do to soften the blow, but at least we'll be there to offer our support."

"Not a real big consolation prize." Kaige shook his head.

"I know, son. Nola is strong, though. You two are already bonded to each other. She'll be okay, if you help her through it like each of you have with the other Hot Rods and their issues. Holden might be a good one to talk to them later tonight, about abandonment and how it can jack up your self-esteem. We'll protect them as best we can from the fallout."

Eli put his hand on Kaige's shoulder. The Hot Rods had leaned on each other enough to know they could survive anything as long as they stuck together. This time would be no different. It wouldn't be pretty. Eventually, it would be okay.

An open wound, then a scab, and someday only a scar that would fade with time.

"Once the girls won't be blindsided by contact with him, we can take them to Steven's place. The rest is up to them."

Tom shrugged, sounding a hell of a lot more confident in the plan of attack he'd outlined than he felt about executing it. "If they want him to be part of their lives, I don't think we should discourage it."

"Until he screws them over again." Kaige looked at Tom like he was crazy.

"People *can* change, Nova."

"That dude knew all along that his family was out there. He never once went to find them to make things right. I don't think he's reformed one bit." Bryce agreed with his fellow mechanic.

"I think you're letting your feelings for Willie cloud your judgment, Dad." A sad smile curved Eli's mouth upward. "It's easy to miss the obvious signs when you're twisted up in how much you want someone."

Everyone knew Eli had done exactly that when he realized he loved both Alanso and Sally. While he'd thought he was making the responsible decision by pushing them away, he'd ended up nearly losing them both before he figured out the right path around the tricky situation.

He was speaking from experience.

"Hey, Tom?" Bryce asked quietly.

"Yeah?"

"We've gone through some serious shit together. You've always been the calm one. Is that why you're so fucked up right now? Where do you think this leaves you and Willie?" he wondered.

"Hell if I know. I love her. I told her so. What I want hasn't changed, but I won't blame her if she can't say the same." He was glad for the sunglasses he wore, which kept his boys from seeing the sheen in his eyes. "She was so skittish about starting a relationship in the first place. What's this going to do to her? Right when she was about to take a leap of faith?"

"The way I see it," Eli growled, "this bastard left her high and dry, with bigots circling around like great whites at a shipwreck."

Kaige jumped in. "I can tell you, I'd *never* ditch Nola and Ambrose if I thought someone might try to hurt them. That's unforgivable. Ms. Brown will feel the same way, Tom. There's no way she could see it differently. Not as a parent. Even if she could forgive the guy for what he did to her personally."

"I think that's probably true." Bryce went for a weak smile. It wasn't very convincing.

"See, Rebel, you were separated from the love of your life for years." Tom knew he was right when Bryce winced. "It didn't change how you felt about her when you finally saw her again. Kaelyn was able to overlook your abandonment, though I admit you had no choice in the matter. Who's to say Willie won't do the same? She has an enormous heart. It's one of the things I love most about her."

"Shit, I thought you loved her cookies best," Eli said, lightening the mood.

"And by cookies, he means her *cookies*." Kaige cupped his fingers on his chest then wiggled his hands up and down as if bouncing his imaginary breasts before strutting a few paces away, swinging his hips.

"Dude. *Never* do that again." Bryce shoved Nova, knocking him onto one of the nearby chaises.

Tom laughed.

It was either that or cry.

They took a while to calm each other down with familiar

routines—jokes, lighthearted teasing, and some roughhousing. After a while, he figured he couldn't delay any further.

"All right, you dumbasses. Let's quit screwing around and make this happen." Tom pushed to his feet.

"I'm coming with you, Dad." Eli stared at him as if daring him to refuse. "I'll stay outside. But you should have someone there in case you need some backup. Besides, you shouldn't drive distracted."

The other guys were quiet as he considered it then nodded. "Thanks."

"Of course." Eli impressed Tom again with how good of a man he'd turned out to be.

Like most well-laid plans, however, they never got a chance to implement theirs. Because just then Tom's phone rang. He glanced at the screen.

Willie.

When he connected the line and said hello, there wasn't an answer. He heard heavy breathing, and not the fun kind. Was she calling to tell him she'd had enough?

Then a thready facsimile of Willie's usual lovely voice interrupted his dread with something far worse than he could have imagined. "I'm at my house. There's someone outside…"

"Son of a bitch! I'm on my way." He jumped to his feet and sprinted down the stairs, his kids right behind without having to be told. Their reckless driving would come in handy right now.

Tom and Eli hopped into his gleaming blue Shelby Cobra while Kaige followed, riding shotgun with Bryce in his Rebel AMC. They had a one-time pass on peeling out when they slammed the pedals to the floors in their ridiculously overpowered vehicles.

They couldn't get him there soon enough.

"Give me your phone," he shouted to Eli.

With his free hand, he dialed Rick. "Where is that piece of shit?!"

"Damn it, Tom. I was watching the house. Something was off. I checked around and saw the root cellar open. I think he nabbed the neighbor's car." The investigator cursed. "It's only been about forty minutes since I saw him for sure. I'm almost to Middletown. Is he at Hot Rods?"

"Worse, he's at Willie's house." Tom's throat nearly closed.

"I'm an exit away from her neighborhood," Rick shouted. "I'll be there in two and a half minutes, tops."

"Don't let anything happen to her," Tom begged then severed the connection so he could try to reassure Willie on the other phone. Except when he lifted it to his ear again, she was gone.

Hang on, Willie. I'm coming.

≋EIGHT

Willie groaned and stretched, her spine screaming and her hip sore from where it had dug into the floor of Tom's living room. That damn man was nowhere to be seen. Again.

"Tommy," she called sleepily.

No answer.

She glanced around the blanket she had slept on and the kitchen table, finding no notes either. Damn if she would wait around again all day, pretending she didn't know something was dreadfully wrong. They were supposed to be partners, damn it.

When she shot to her feet to snatch her dress off the floor, pain stabbed her head. She went to her knees and grabbed her skull, hoping to keep it from bursting.

This affair with Tom London would be the death of her. Maybe she'd been right to stay away. Tears accumulated in her eyes as she fumbled for the pill bottles they'd left nearby. She shook out the proper dosages then swallowed them dry.

As much as she would like to go over and say good morning to her daughter and grandbaby, she wouldn't risk running into Tom or cornering him into talking about a relationship he clearly wasn't able to handle yet. If ever.

She shoveled her medicine into her purse, slipped on her clothes and shoes, then stumbled out of the house, locking the door behind her. Standing on the front porch, she looked back, blinking rapidly, her lips and chin trembling as she wondered if she'd ever stay there again.

If not, she'd find a way to move on. She had before.

Putting her shoulders back, she marched to her car then drove across town to her dinky, half-abandoned house. She flew upstairs and started running steamy water for a bath, which never failed to calm her. As she soaked in the rich, foamy bubbles Amber and Nola had given her for her last birthday, she wondered when she'd become a quitter.

She'd never have tolerated that kind of defeatist attitude from her girls.

So why should it be good enough for her?

It wasn't.

Almost an hour of thinking brought her to one conclusion.

She had her heart set on Tom London and she'd make him see that despite whatever craziness he'd cooked up to psych himself out, they were meant to be together. When logic wouldn't work, sexy lingerie might.

Willie grinned as she finished her bath then took forever fixing her hair and even putting on some of the makeup she'd bought from one of the neighbors who moonlighted selling cosmetics. Of course, she'd never planned to use the stuff, except as a way to support the single mother who busted her ass to provide for her children without offending her with a straight-up handout.

Then she sauntered naked to her closet and rummaged around in the way, way back.

At first, she couldn't find what she was searching for. Had she gotten rid of it? Donated it years ago and forgotten?

Then her fingers brushed against lace and satin. She grinned.

It was a negligee set she'd hand sewn for one of her clients. Supposed to be the woman's wedding-night wear. Except the guy she'd been about to marry cheated on her. Willie had offered to waive her fees. The woman had insisted on paying, with her fiancé's money, then refused to accept her purchase.

Some of Willie's best work slipped through her fingers as she admired the piece all over again. She remembered how she'd tried it on once, knowing the woman was nearly exactly her size. Maybe it had been wishful thinking that had made her hang on to it, or simply pride in her labor, but she thought it would make a persuasive argument in her case to Tom.

She wasn't against fighting dirty to convince him of what was best for them both.

Willie grinned as she stepped into the sexy garment. When she'd wrestled the various straps, white-satin panels, and matching lace-topped garters into place, she peered at herself in her full-length mirror, turning this way then that.

Pretty damn fine if she did say so herself.

Especially when matched up with the silver high heels she'd worn to Nola's wedding.

She'd only barely headed back toward the closet to find a

low-cut dress that she usually wore with a camisole beneath—though she wouldn't today—when a noise from downstairs caught her attention.

Could it be that stray cat scratching at the window again? She'd love to feed the poor thing, and invite it inside, but the landlord was a hardass about his no-pets rule.

Just this once, she felt like leading a revolt.

It was amazing the power a proper set of undergarments could lend a lady.

She chuckled to herself as she snuck down the stairs.

Instead of the cat she'd expected to see, a man's face obscured most of the living room window. His hand pressed to the pane above his forehead, allowing him to peep farther into her home.

Her fingers flew to her chest. She instinctively recoiled, falling on her ass on the stairs with a yelp. The noise drew the man's attention. When he caught sight of her, his eyes widened and he disappeared. She thought he had run for it, busted spying into what probably seemed like a deserted house.

Not taking any chances, she dashed down the stairs, retrieved her phone from the table near the door where she'd dropped it, her purse, and her keys when she'd come in.

The sharp rap on the sidelight nearly made her shoot through the roof.

Willie shrieked as she multitasked. With her right hand, she swiped the screen of her phone, looking for someone to call. Sure, she should have gone for 911. Except, when it came right down to it, she didn't hesitate to tap the icon representing Tom. No matter what was screwed up between them, he would come when she needed help. It was a gut instinct and she went with it.

Simultaneously, she grabbed the wooden baseball bat Amber had insisted they keep in case of intruders. Though she didn't relish the idea of bashing in someone's skull, she'd do what she had to in order to keep herself safe.

Her daughters needed her. Ambrose, too. Most of all, so did Tom.

Maybe now more than ever.

"Willie? Willie?" Tom's voice grew louder and more urgent when she didn't answer him right away.

Without bringing the phone to her ear, she said, as calmly and quickly as she could manage, "I'm at my house. There's someone outside. A man. Peeping in the windows and trying to get in."

The doorknob rattled and she screamed.

"Are you okay?" The voice from outside seemed sort of familiar yet sort of not. *"Wilhelmina!"*

She dropped the phone. It skittered away, landing under a bench in their cramped entryway.

Only one person had ever said her name quite like that.

It couldn't be.

"Wilhelmina! Open up. It's me…*Steven.*"

If her head hadn't already been spinning by that point, a specter trying to invade her house would have done it for sure. She collapsed to her knees, trying to draw a single deep breath when all she could manage were short, fast pants that had her on the verge of blacking out in seconds.

"Answer me, please." The man outside pounded. "It sounded like you fell, baby. Tell me you're okay?"

She couldn't, because she wasn't.

A loud thump came at the door. The cheap wood flexed in front of her eyes.

Another crash followed, this time causing splinters to appear around the deadbolt.

Willie crab-walked backward, the bat forgotten as a third kick busted in her front door.

It flew open, smashing the mirror behind it.

As glass rained around her—slicing her arm and maybe her legs too, she couldn't tell—a man stepped through the wreckage of her home, and her sanity. It couldn't possibly be him.

But it was.

"Wilhelmina!" Steven charged through the debris and skidded beside her on his knees. He bundled her into his arms while she fought him viciously. Punching, kicking, screaming, and generally acting like that wildcat outside when it ran into another kitty poaching on his turf.

Because if Steven was here then everything she'd ever believed was a lie.

"Calm down, baby." He took a few hits to his face, including one pretty good shot from her elbow that started a bright red streak running from his nose. "I can explain everything. Please, let me talk to you."

His voice had some roughness to it that she didn't think came from his distress, but rather from age. So often, she'd imagined what he'd look like if he'd survived that damn car crash. Never had she pictured so many wrinkles and droops in his face, which had already blackened from her impacts.

He hadn't aged gracefully, not like Tom.

Every inch of him seemed worn and slouched, as if he'd carried a heavy burden the past twenty years. Maybe he had.

"That's better, baby," he crooned as her initial terror faded to awe.

"It's you," she rasped. "It's *really* you?"

She turned in his hold, running her fingers along the body she should have known well. He was a stranger to her now. So different from the young man she'd lived with.

It wasn't only that he was older. He seemed…weak. Manipulative with a sprinkle of nutty as he smiled down at her like everything was perfect now that they'd been reunited.

In a flash, she compared him to Tom London and—in every way—found him lacking.

"It is."

"How can this be?" She needed to know that all those years of misery weren't for nothing.

Instead of answering, he raked his gaze over her body, from her breasts—pushed up high by the boning of her teddy—to her sexy shoes. Willie wanted nothing more than to cover herself from his appraising stare.

"Damn, baby. Did you know I was coming? Did that guy Tom tell you already?" Steven leaned in and put his lips on hers.

Willie wrenched free of his grasp and swung hard, slapping him across his foul, delusional mouth.

Which was exactly when Tom barreled through the door, a step ahead of his investigator friend, Rick.

"Get your motherfucking hands off of her." Tom grabbed Steven by the throat and lifted him from the floor, slamming him against the wall near the broken mirror. "Do you like feeling my knuckles in your face or what, asshole?"

So it hadn't been her elbow that had given him that black eye after all.

She should have known.

Last night. Tom. The hole in the wall. Every damn thing. It suddenly made sense.

And here she was, dressed like a fool, surrounded by men who'd played her like a pawn in the game of her own life.

Willie put her hand on the floor and attempted to stand, falling twice before she managed it. Tom dropped Steven, shoving him toward Kaige, Bryce, and Eli, who piled inside, blocking any hope of escape through the wreckage of her door.

She touched her head, trying to slow the spinning of the room around her.

Tom was there, wrapping her in his arms.

But she wasn't sure that's what she wanted.

"You knew?" She hated that the question sounded more like a whimper.

"Found out yesterday." He groaned. "I don't expect you to believe me, but I was on my way over here to tell you when you called."

That explained how they got there so damn quickly, not that she was complaining.

"I didn't want you to hear it from someone else, Wilhelmina," Steven yelled from where Eli had her husband's arms pinned behind him, none too gently.

"You hurt her," Kaige roared, his legendary temper surfacing without Nola to calm him down. "Haven't you done that enough already? Now she's scared and bleeding, too. You should have left this job to someone who actually loves her."

"I *do* love you." Steven stared at her as he spoke. He wouldn't shut up despite the hostile welcoming committee surrounding him. "I always have. Everything I did was for you. And the girls."

"Don't you fucking dare mention *my wife*," Kaige snarled. "If you'd given a single fuck about her or her sister, you never would have left them to fend for themselves. You deserve to suffer, like they did."

"Nova," Willie called. "Thank you, but it's okay. *I'm* okay."

Every man in the place, Steven included, threw her a skeptical glance.

"I will be. Take a walk and cool off, please."

"For the record, this will never be okay by me." Kaige looked at Willie. "This is bullshit. I hope you don't believe a word out of his lying mouth when we both know what's best for you."

Bryce ushered his garagemate outside. With Eli holding Steven, and Rick keeping guard, he wasn't going anywhere.

Plus, there were fewer witnesses to her shame and unraveling this way, which she appreciated. As if he sensed her discomfort, Tom took off his shirt. He held it out to her then helped her thread her arms through it until soft cotton warmed by his skin shielded her from Steven's view.

He pressed on the slice across her upper arm to stop the bleeding, using the shirt he'd just given her as a bandage. The world began to come into better focus with him nearby.

"That's it, honey." He rubbed her back. "Take a deep breath and hold it for me, will you?"

She did as he asked.

"Okay, now again."

A few more and she was feeling her temporary relief morphing into disgust and anger. Her fists balled at her sides and she took a couple wobbly steps toward Steven.

Tom put his arm around her waist and steadied her. He didn't dare try to stop her.

Rick rocked onto the balls of his feet, ready to spring between Steven and her, or maybe Steven and Tom, if necessary.

Willie put up her hand, disgusted by the shakiness of her fingers when she traced first the fiery handprint she'd left on Steven's cheek and then the serious black eye he was sporting.

"It's really you?" Every few seconds her mind seemed to reset and she needed to remind herself it was true. Sort of like after he'd died and she kept expecting him to walk through the door anyway.

"Yes." He smiled at her as if she'd forgiven him.

"Then you'd better start explaining pretty *fucking* quick," she snapped.

Beside her, Tom gasped. She never cursed. If only Quinn was there to lecture her about it. She nearly laughed hysterically, on the verge of losing her mind.

"Okay. Short version. I faked the accident. To protect you. And the girls. I thought you'd get money to run somewhere safe. Nothing seems to have worked out the way I planned, but I'm here now and I want to make it up to you. To them. I've missed you every single day of the past twenty-one years, Wilhelmina."

This time it was Steven who started sobbing.

She couldn't bring herself to care about his misery. He certainly hadn't weighed hers or their children's very heavily in his actions.

"You're saying you *chose* to leave us?" She tipped her head to the side, his words not fully computing in her dazed mind.

"No!" He shook his head violently, flinging tears and snot and blood in the process. "What choice did I have? What else could I have done?"

"I can think of about fifty options off the top of my head."

Eli jumped in to protect Willie as if he were her own flesh and blood.

"You've got no idea what it's like to live terrified of finding your family dead," Steven snapped at Eli.

"Wrong." Willie wouldn't allow her husband, ex-husband, to take a swipe at the young man. "He's suffered worse. He *did* lose his mother. Just like I grieved for the man I thought I loved."

"I'm right here, Wilhelmina."

"No. You were obviously never the man I thought you were." She looked at Eli, then Rick. "Get him out of my sight."

"I made a mistake!" Steven yelled as they dragged him down the stairs then along the cracked sidewalk toward the cars parked haphazardly on the lawn. "I love you, Wilhelmina. I want you back. I'll be waiting. Whenever you're ready."

"I wish I could slam that door in his face right now," she bitched to no one in particular.

Tom's laugh was strained.

As soon as Eli and Rick shoved Steven in the car and hauled him away like the garbage he was, it was as if she lost the sheer willpower keeping her upright. She slumped against Tom.

"Whoa, Willie." He was there to catch her before she fell, scooping her into his arms. "It's all right. You're safe."

"Oh, God. What will the girls think when they find out?" Willie couldn't handle the thought of the pain she knew she wouldn't be able to spare her daughters. If it hurt even a fraction of how badly Steven had stabbed her, she knew it would be devastating.

"One thing at a time, honey. How are you? What do you want me to do?" Tom held her close and rocked her.

She'd never appreciated his consideration more than right

then. Better, he was giving her the ability to control her destiny—unlike Steven, who'd made every important life-changing decision in isolation then left her to live with the consequences.

"Take me to Hot Rods."

"Okay, sure," he whispered then laid the barest of kisses on her forehead. "Anything you want, Willie. I'll do it for you."

He carried her outside. Bryce and Kaige noticed and held the door to the Rebel as Tom climbed inside, without once letting go of her. Not even when the first sob bubbled from her chest.

She looked up at him in horror. The storm of emotions wouldn't blow over quickly once she let it bluster.

"It's okay, Willie. Let it out. I've got you."

Another hiccup turned into a choked wail. Then another and another followed, each one turning into more hideous cries.

Somewhere beyond her grief, both for the man she'd lost and the younger version of herself—who'd been too gullible to see the truth—she heard Bryce say softly, "We love you, Ms. Brown. Don't forget, Hot Rods are for life."

Could she deserve to be one of them? Could she risk her heart again after having it stomped on so brutally? Especially now that she knew how much more powerful her link to Tom was? If it broke, it would destroy her.

She didn't know if she could be that stupidly brave. And she was afraid it wouldn't only be her that got hurt if she couldn't rebuild herself yet again. Tears poured down her cheeks. Selfish, she couldn't help but accept the Hot Rods' comfort anyway, especially Tom's.

Willie curled against his chest and let every emotion swirling around her vent through her frenzied sobbing. She wasn't sure if it was because she couldn't catch her breath, or because the racking of her body exacerbated the throb in her brain, or because her soul simply couldn't withstand any more shredding, but midnight descended early, enveloping her in its comforting cloak of nothingness.

"Oh, shit. She's gonna pass out." Tom urged Kaige, "Drive faster, let's get her home."

Home.

Was that where she belonged? How could she ever trust herself, and her judgment in love again?

She was afraid she'd lost another place, and the people along with it, before she'd ever really had them.

Could it be that she was destined to be alone?

NINE

Tom sat up in bed for the second sleepless night in a row. His shoulders rested against his headboard while Willie lay beside him, her head in his lap. He ran his fingers through her hair, then along her shoulder and up her back in an endless circuit that hopefully soothed her half as much as it was doing for him.

She slept in her sexy negligee since he hadn't wanted to risk waking her while trying to unravel the getup.

Looking like a centerfold angel, she couldn't possibly have been more heartbreakingly beautiful. Except maybe for the butterfly bandage holding the slice on her upper arm closed. Should he have taken her for stitches?

The last thing he wanted was for Steven to give her another scar to bear. Tom couldn't help but wonder if she'd already slipped through his fingers, like her silky curls did. In tune with her every breath, he noticed when the pattern of her respiration changed.

Willie shifted, then blinked a couple times.

When she saw him awake, guarding her, she tried to talk.

A husky whisper was all she could manage. "Tommy?"

"Yeah." He smiled at her, helping her to sit up some before leaning to the side to grab the glass of water he'd left on his nightstand in case she needed to take her medicine again. "Here, have a sip."

Her throat must have been raw after the way she'd screamed at her husband, first fending him off then confronting him directly and finally when she'd cried herself out in Tom's arms.

"Thanks." She offered him a weak smile after chugging the entire glass. "I had the *weirdest* dream…"

Tom tried to school his face into a blank mask. He knew he'd failed utterly when she tensed in his hold and tried to scoot away. "It was real?"

"Ah, shit." He brought her closer instead, hugging her until she subdued her fight-or-flight reaction to the adrenaline that must have spiked in her upon realizing, again, that Steven had abandoned her rather than dying that night on the side of the road.

She elbowed Tom in the ribs, making him ease up on his clutch. Though she didn't go far, she backed away enough to allow her to grab his hands and study them. Eventually, she declared, "His face looked worse."

Tom couldn't help it. He laughed despite the dirty look she shot him.

"Forgive me if I don't crack up with you, Tommy." Her chin

raised and her shoulders went back. "What the hell were you thinking by keeping that from me last night? I sure as shit would have rather heard it from you than find out like I did. Did you think you could hide it forever?"

He shook his head. She didn't let him speak.

"Because that makes you not much better than…*him*." It was as if she couldn't bring herself to say the guy's name anymore. She stood. "I think I'd better go home."

"Willie, wait." He grabbed her fingers and kept her from fleeing. "You can't. Your door is busted and—"

"Okay, fine. I'll go to Hot Rods. Or to stay with Amber and Gavyn." She stared him down. "Tom London, you let go of my hand right this instant."

Swallowing hard, he did as she demanded. "Honey, I'm not trying to bully you. I'm only afraid that you might not be thinking clearly after such a shock. I'll take you anywhere safe you want to go. Okay? Just let me put some pants on and I'll do anything that makes this easier for you. That's all I want. You, happy."

"Well, crap." She deflated, sinking onto the edge of the bed once more. "It's hard to argue when you have to be so stinking reasonable."

Tom smiled, relief flooding him. "Good to know."

Willie sat there, still, for so long, he wasn't sure what to do next. So he patted the space beside him on the mattress. "It's toasty over here. You must be chilly since you're hardly wearing anything."

"I think this outfit must be cursed." She plucked at one of the stockings.

He might have asked her what she meant by that if she hadn't taken him up on his offer.

Scooting closer, she leaned against his side, laying her cheek on his shoulder. "What am I going to do, Tommy?"

His heart fractured, mostly because he didn't know what to tell her. What he wanted and what was best for her might be completely opposite. He manned up and told the truth. "I understand if you want to get back together with him. Steven was the love of your life. And while I completely disagree with his actions, maybe he's not the same guy anymore. If you want to talk to him, I'd go with you. Or arrange for Rick to sit at a table nearby somewhere public. I don't think you should go alone, or meet him in private though. I'm sorry. I don't trust him worth a fuck."

To her credit, Willie didn't deny the suggestion in some reflexive reaction, nor did she jump on the opportunity. She really thought about it. For so long he wasn't sure she planned to say anything else until morning.

Eventually, though, she did. "What would you do? If you could have Michelle back?"

"Hmm." Dead tired, he responded without quite thinking his answer through. "I'd probably take a page out of the kids' playbook and see if you two were down with a ménage."

Hey, it was honest.

Willie slapped his thigh then cracked up. She laughed and laughed until he worried she might have gone off the deep end. Tears spilled down her cheeks and though they were borne of amusement, he couldn't help but remember what it had been like when she sobbed in his arms earlier.

What if that *was* their solution. Could he give her something like that with a dude he didn't respect? "Uh…honey…if that's what you want, I'm not sure if I could—"

"Oh my God, Tom London. Stop. Right. There." She clutched her stomach as another round of giggles consumed her. "Or I'm going to pee in your bed."

"Let's not do that." He frowned. What's so damn funny?

"Sorry, sorry." She patted his hand. "It's that I'm so angry, I can't imagine how you think I'd go back to him. Or expect you to…"

Then she looked up at him with questioning eyes. "Why would you want me to be with a man like that? Because I made the mistake of trusting him forever ago? No, I won't be that foolish ever again."

"You're right." Tom nodded. "*I* don't want you with him. But if that's what you want, then I'll do my best not to beat him to a pulp and help you get whatever it will take to make you happy."

She sighed, making her breasts nearly overflow the contraption pushing them up so prettily. "I could never care for him the same way again. Besides, the man I married may still be alive, but *his* wife… Well, she's gone. Forever. I'm not that gullible, innocent, fragile woman anymore. And the thing that pisses me off the most about this debacle… Okay, maybe not the most, but right up there… The one I keep coming back to…is the fact that you weren't sure if I could handle this."

"You gotta cut me a break, honey. I was pretty fucking floored myself when I heard the news. I wanted to take more than ten shitty minutes to calm down and think logically about how best to tell you so that I didn't hurt you any more than I knew I had to." He scrubbed his hand over his face. "I know there's no way I can prove it to you, but I was seriously on my way to your place."

"I believed you when you told me before. You're not a liar. And I noticed you got there awfully quickly."

"Eli drove." He shrugged one shoulder as if that explained everything. It pretty much did.

Willie mulled things over for a while. He took it as a good sign that she left her hand on his leg, where it had landed earlier. Her thumb rubbed slightly back and forth while she debated his fate.

"In the morning, will you go with me to talk to Nola and Amber?" Her breathing hitched at the thought alone.

"Of course." Tom cradled her fingers and brought them to his lips to kiss them lightly.

"Thank you." She looked up at him then. "For coming to rescue me, and for staying by my side. For your unwavering support. If it's not too much, there's one more thing I'd like to ask of you."

"Anything, Willie."

"Make love to me."

# TEN

Tom couldn't believe he'd heard Willie correctly. "You mean…
Now? You want to, after everything that's happened?"

"Is that a problem?" She worried her lip. "I need to stop
dwelling on it for a while myself. Shut off my mind and just feel.
Has this made you think less of me, for being so naive?"

"What?" He reared back. "Hell no. If anything, I admire
you. I don't know if I'd still be standing after a shock like that."

"Technically, I'm mostly lying down." She smiled ruefully.
"Come on, Tommy. I have no one to be loyal to anymore. Not
even a memory. I mean, not that I think you should feel the
same way about Michelle."

"It's okay, I know what you meant. I'm at peace with things,
Willie."

Then her eyes narrowed. "Where's your necklace?"

"I put it away," he told her. "I didn't want anything standing
between us or our future anymore. Then this happened…"

He shrugged.

"Wow, it's been a crazy couple of days." She sighed, seeming as if she might shatter if anything else hit her.

"Why don't you roll over? Let me help you relax." He thought of the massage oils he'd stashed in his nightstand earlier in the week. He hadn't gotten to end their picnic the way he wanted the day before, but he could make up for it now. "Whatever happens after that, we'll go with it."

"Mmm," she moaned softly as she did as he requested.

"Tell me one thing?" he asked as he retrieved the cinnamon gel that had reminded him of her post-baking spiciness.

"What?" She peeked over her shoulder as she settled onto her stomach.

Her ass looked fucking fantastic in the delicate panties and garters she still wore.

"Was this outfit supposed to be for me?"

She laughed, making her lush curves jiggle some, which did absolutely nothing to dissuade him from the course they'd set. "Uh-huh."

"Damn. Even though I was acting like an idiot?" He knelt, sticking the bottle behind him in the crook of his bent leg to warm up while he traced the straps that ran from her stockings upward.

"I was planning to help you wise up," she said with enough sass that he would have smacked her ass if it had been any other time.

"I feel like a genius right now." He teased her instead. "And I think it's only fair that I get a turn to explore every inch of you. Maybe tomorrow, or some other time, you could model this for me again. I almost hate to take it off."

"Or I could create another set. With all these lovebirds around, they've had me wonder lately if I shouldn't start my own line of custom lingerie."

"Hang on, you *made* this?" He traced the edges of the wicked ensemble, drawing a sigh from her in the process.

"Yep." She nodded slightly, rubbing her cheek over her forearm, where it was pillowed.

"Damn, woman. You're talented. Beautiful, smart, funny, and tough, too."

"Hmm. I don't feel so strong right now." Her lips curved into a frown that made him want to kiss it away. So he did.

And when he'd finished showering her with tender rubs of his lips over hers, he said, "You're holding yourself to an unrealistic standard. There are a lot of people who wouldn't have been able to deal with the kind of surprise you got today."

"I'm not sure if I can still. I have to tell the girls." She sniffled and tensed. "Oh, Tommy. What am I going to say to them?"

"Hush." He kissed her cheek then resumed his feather-light caresses over her arms, back, and legs. "We'll figure that out tomorrow. It's been twenty-one years. A few more hours won't matter. Tonight, let me take care of you."

Willie didn't argue.

So Tom began to undress her, beginning with the row of hook and eyes that held her teddy closed. One by one, he unfastened them, kissing the rich skin he revealed with each flick. When he reached the final one, he spread the material wide on either side of her and marveled at the expanse of her naked back.

From the softly rounded ridges of her shoulder blades, to the valley of her spine and the hills that began where her dainty waist flared to her ass, he adored every bit of the landscape of her body. He worked on showing her precisely how much when he kissed her all over while gliding his hands across her soft skin.

When she arched upward to maintain contact with his mouth as he skimmed across her, he fit one hand beneath her to rest on her stomach, then lifted her enough that he could remove the top section of her masterpiece from her entirely.

Tom set her down, this time directly on his soft, fuzzy sheets. She sighed and snuggled deeper into them, rubbing her breasts and belly in the spot he usually slept.

Unable to help himself, Tom leaned down and bit her lightly on the side of her ass as he freed her stockings from the suspenders holding them high up on her legs. Once they were free, he situated himself between her knees. He rolled the white silk stocking down her thigh and calf before tossing it to the floor. Then he repeated the slow caress on her other side.

By the time her toes were exposed, they curled, giving him a peek at her pale-pink nail polish. Everything about her appealed to him. That hint of femininity included.

Finally, he addressed her panties. Carefully, so as not to rip a single stitch of her handiwork, he tugged them over the fullest part of her ass then worked them off her legs.

She was nude and completely willing before him.

Tom could have roared, or beat his chest, with the overwhelming need to claim her that rushed though him. However, he hadn't cruised along for the past year only to rush now. Not without making this the best possible experience Willie could have.

After meeting Steven, and knowing what Tom did now, he

figured he could show her an entirely different kind of loving than she might have been accustomed to in the past.

From his place between her knees, he could clearly see the paler folds of her pussy between her legs, and while he might have done almost anything for a taste of her, he had other things to do first.

Tom retrieved the body-temperature oil from beneath his leg. He flipped open the cap and poured a generous amount into his palms. After washing his hands in the stuff, and enjoying the slight tingle it gave his fingers, he picked up one of Willie's feet.

He rubbed, lightly at first then harder, using his thumbs to press the pad near her toes, then her arch, and finally her heel.

She moaned when he repeated the motion a few times.

"Feel good?" he asked.

"So good I'm not sure if I want you to keep doing that or stop and skip to the better stuff." She chuckled.

He did, too.

His cock voted for the better stuff.

No problems in that department tonight.

Older and wiser than he might have been in his younger days, Tom stayed the course. He would take his time. An hour or more massaging her, until she couldn't stand being touched for how much arousal he'd inspired in her, would be to his benefit in the long run.

It turned into a game for him, to see how high he could take her.

And he wasn't a man who liked to lose.

He braceleted the fine bones of her ankle, rubbing them carefully as his other hand undulated over the top of her foot.

Gradually, he moved upward, caressing her calf before allowing his thumbs to knead the muscles there. Graceful yet strong, they resisted at first. Then eventually turned pliant in his hold.

Bit by bit, he relaxed her.

Her thigh took longer, making him press deeper and use more oil to coat her enough to glide across her skin. She glimmered in the moonlight, making him think of an onyx mermaid or a skinny-dipper come to visit him from a warm summer night's dip.

When he reached the bottom swell of her ass, he paused, making her groan in frustration.

"Can't leave you uneven, Willie." He *tsked* before scooting backwards and beginning over again with her other foot, paying special attention to her prettily painted toes. This time, when he reached her ass, he didn't restrain himself. He leaned forward, placing a kiss on each cheek before taking the bottle of oil and drizzling it over her until he imagined what it might look like if he were to ice her ass with his come.

He'd have to try that one day soon.

Tom snuck his fingers inside his briefs and used his oiled hand to stroke himself a few times from root to tip. The ache she caused in his balls made him sure his release would be epic. No way would he find that pleasure anywhere except inside her tonight.

With a hiss, he pried his fingers from his shaft and resumed where he'd left off, paying special attention to the deep tissue of her knotted muscles. Willie groaned and her legs parted a tiny bit more when the tension she carried there released. Though he was tempted to slip his hand between the tops of her thighs and slide his fingers into her pussy, he restrained himself.

"Tom," she whispered.

"Not yet. Soak it in, Willie. I'm going to build you higher," he insisted then let his hands roam up to her waist, his fingers contracting where her body grew narrower. He pressed, allowing his weight to transfer to the heels of his palms as Kayla Rosewood, masseuse and owner of Bare Natural, had shown him when they'd visited the Powertools crew for the recent Hot Rods' wedding.

He spent a long time working on her back, trailing his hands down either side of her spine before gliding up her sides on constant repeat. His muscles burned with the effort, though he never would have complained. Blood pumped through his entire body, priming him for the outlet he would allow himself as a reward for a job well done.

Much later.

Next he concentrated on her neck. Kissing her nape as he pushed her thick hair to one side. Her lids fluttered, but she breathed so deeply and slowly, he thought he might have put her to sleep again.

His cock nearly revolted in his shorts. But if he could grant her a few hours of serenity, he wouldn't mind. When he paused simply to admire her, her eyes opened a bit. "Don't stop. Please."

Utterly relaxed, she looked like a different person. One who didn't have to watch her own back constantly. He hoped he saw this side of her more often.

Tom kissed her cheek, then the curve of her forehead facing him. "Wouldn't dare."

He moved on to her shoulders, drawing a few groans from her.

Some time later, he progressed to her arms, rubbing first

one then the other from the tops all the way to her fingertips, careful not to reopen the slash from the broken mirror. He paid special attention to her hands, wondering how she got the faint scar on her thumb and cataloging the fine wrinkles around her knuckles that proclaimed her a survivor.

It was better to grow old gracefully than the alternative—not getting there at all—he figured. The proof of her struggles to stay in the game only made him respect her more. When he'd imprinted himself on every bit of her he could reach, he nudged her hip.

"Flip over."

Rubber-limbed, she could hardly budge.

They laughed softly together when she resembled a newborn kitten with her uncoordinated efforts. So Tom helped her, rotating her until she lay on her back and smiled softly up at him.

"Hi," she murmured.

"I hope you don't mind if I stare at you for a minute." He could hardly breathe with his chest tightening so much.

"Take two." Her smile widened. "It's nice to know you enjoy the scenery."

He swallowed, hoping his tongue wasn't lolling out of his mouth as he admired her breasts, which may not have been perky, but made up for it in fullness and softness and pure loveliness. The stretch marks on her stomach were like badges of honor, proclaiming her a mother of two of the most wonderful young ladies on the planet.

Hardly allowing his gaze to skim her pussy, for fear he'd lose the lingering scraps of his control, he tipped his head back then clenched his jaw. "If I liked the way you looked any more, I'd be coming in my pants."

"Technically," she said, "You're not wearing any. But your underwear is blocking my view."

He laughed. "That's my insurance policy."

"Against?"

He licked his lips. "Fucking you before we're ready."

"I couldn't possibly be more ready, Tommy." She lifted her hips toward him in invitation.

"I'll be the judge of that. If you really want though, I'll lose the briefs."

"I do," she purred.

He yanked them down and off so quickly, he might as well have shredded them Hulk-style. Well, if there was a Hulk who ripped off his clothes out of lust instead of anger, he supposed.

His cock hung heavy between his thighs, his balls feeling as dense as lug nuts as they dangled free. Willie hummed her approval then reached for him.

Quickly, he caught her wrists then pinned them to the bed beside her. "None of that, honey, or I won't make it to the main event."

"At this rate, I'm going to be a senior citizen before the show starts, Tommy," she teased, the glint in her eye proving she didn't mind.

"Then quit distracting me so I can finish the job here."

She seemed as if she might argue more until he slathered her entire body with the rest of the oil, emptying the bottle onto her breasts, belly, and even her mound, slicking the neatly trimmed patch of hair there.

His hands followed the trail he'd left for them, smearing her with the delicious-smelling goo as he caressed each part of her. Of course he cheated when he plumped her breasts, brushing first his thumbs and then his lips over the pebbled nipples. A few shades darker than the rest of her skin, they reminded him of expensive dark chocolate.

Once he began tasting her, there was no stopping himself. He drew her flesh into his mouth and laved it with the flat of his tongue, making her cry out at the contact. Pausing, he lifted his head to meet her heavy-lidded gaze. "Shh, Willie. I'm going to give you everything you need, I promise. Enjoy this."

"Tommy." She put her hands on his shoulders and tugged him closer to her once more.

"Yes, ma'am." He got back to work as she demanded.

As he suckled at her breasts, he let his hands wander over her body, petting her everywhere he'd missed. Everywhere, except *there*.

When he skimmed past her pussy, she protested, squirming beneath him mindlessly. Still he resisted, using his thumbs in mirror images to finish massaging her quads. Only when he'd done as thorough a job as he could manage did he let himself release her breast with one final tug of his lips to begin kissing a path along the center of her body toward her core.

He slithered downward, lowering himself between her legs until his cock was trapped almost painfully beneath his body. He might as well have been balanced on a tailpipe, considering how steely his shaft was. Unable to stop himself, he rutted against the mattress a few times then growled as he scooped his hands beneath Willie's spectacular ass and drew her toward his open mouth.

"Oh, yes," she moaned when his breath washed over her spread pussy.

From this close up, he could clearly see the arousal making her labia glisten and the involuntary flexing of her opening as her body primed itself for his entry. He remembered how tight she'd been around his finger when he'd eaten her on the couch and couldn't wait to feel that taut, humid flesh hugging him again.

So he prodded the ring of muscle at her entrance. The contact of his index finger at her pussy made her clamp down and groan. So sensitive. All right, so he'd laid on the foreplay thick enough to make anyone super-horny. He wasn't sorry.

Nor did he stop applying the steady pressure that had him sinking into her bit by bit.

"Tom!" She screamed his name and surprised the hell out of him by coming before he'd even fully embedded his finger in her channel. Wanting her to get the most out of her orgasm, he dipped his head and sucked lightly on her clit, relishing the spasms of her cunt from the inside.

When her quaking had dulled to shudders, he nuzzled her mound, moving his attention slightly off dead-center while she was recovering. Still, he never stopped the steady in and out motion of his hand or the swirls of his tongue along her glossy folds.

Before long, she moaned, so he kept going. The decadent sound came more frequently and louder as he explored the area between her legs. Leaving no part of her untouched, he stimulated all of her that he could reach with puffs of air, careful rasps of his five o'clock shadow, swipes of his tongue and lips and, of course, his fingers.

Eventually, he added a second to her pussy and allowed his pinky to rub against her back passage while he targeted her clit with his mouth.

"Tommy, wait." She clawed at his shoulders, only spurring him on.

Burying his face against her, he increased the pace of his flickering tongue and his pumping hand.

"I want to come with you," she shouted, her hips rocking up to meet his mouth in betrayal of her wishes.

He paused only long enough to say, "You will. Next time."

"No. Tonight!" She misunderstood.

"Yeah, honey. Next round…or two." He grinned at her and resumed his working of her pussy.

Conflicted, she opened her mouth and moaned, "No." Followed by, "Yes."

He laughed against her, the vibration sealing the deal.

Tom pushed her over the edge into rapture, consuming the arousal that accompanied her ecstasy. Nothing could have tasted sweeter to him.

Except the one thing he hadn't yet had since they'd started this prolonged madness.

Her lips.

He lifted his left arm up and crossed it over in front of his face, wiping the excess moisture from his mouth onto his biceps, loving that she'd soaked him with her pleasure. Then he grinned as he levered himself over her and came eye to eye with the most spectacular woman alive.

"Hey there." He rubbed his nose along hers. "How's it going?"

"Pretty good." Willie laughed then flung her arms around

him. She hauled him against her with deceptive strength. Their chests collided and his deprived skin radiated delight from every cell that came into contact with her.

Tom couldn't help it. He shoved himself against her then back a bit, loving how he glided along the length of her supple body now that she was saturated with oil. His cock nudged her entrance and they both froze as their playfulness turned serious.

Her knees drew up and clasped his hips.

He stared into her eyes, getting lost in the obsidian depths.

And when their mouths met, as if drawn together by some force of nature, he nearly came all over her belly.

Tom jammed a hand between them, strangling the base of his cock. He panted as he scrunched his eyes closed for a few seconds then said, with a wry twist of his lips, "Oops. Might have gotten carried away there."

"I liked it." Willie ran her hands down his back, using those nails of hers to drive him wild while bringing him slightly under control with the edge of pain.

"Do it again," she begged. "But this time…I want you inside me when you kiss me. Please, Tommy. Please."

He nodded, dislodging a couple rogue droplets of sweat from his forehead. The strain of performing for her kept building, though he refused to let either of them down when this encounter had a decent shot at smashing every best-of sex record he'd ever held.

Except here was one thing he wished he knew without asking. "Uh, Willie?"

"*Tommy*, if you back out now—"

"I'm not going anywhere." He grimaced, the insistence of his arousal nearly convincing him to ignore reality for as long as it took to get off. "But... Sorry, I don't know how it works exactly. Should have Googled this shit. Do I still need to use a condom?"

Willie grinned, enjoying his discomfort a teensy bit too much for his male pride to bear.

"Seriously, tell me now or we'll just have to deal with the consequences." His cock already rode the furrow of her pussy as he rubbed the blunt tip against her silky folds.

"You would, yes." She winked at him. "Except I get hormone shots to help me through the transition period. It's safe to be inside me bare."

"Fuck, yes." He reached down and took himself in hand. Aiming his cock, he set the tip at her entrance. "I'll try to go slow. You'll tell me if I hurt you?"

"You could never do that, Tommy." She smiled softly up at him then nudged him toward her so that they could kiss as he finally joined their bodies as closely as their hearts and souls had been for a while, even if neither of them was ready to admit it.

He felt virginal again as he burrowed into her welcoming body, straining to fit himself to her while giving her time to accommodate his length and girth. The initial sensations of pressing within her for their first time overwhelmed him. Perfection.

Willie gasped, and he froze. She refused to surrender that easily though, instead rocking her hips upward to swallow more of his shaft. Not every woman he'd been with had been able to take all of him. She seemed unable to settle for less.

So he gave them both what they desired.

Tom devoured Willie's cries, kissing her deeply as he began to impale her fully with short jabs accompanied by the grind of his hips. His ass flexed, driving him deeper until every inch of his cock was nestled inside her pussy.

Her sheath rippled around him, threatening to milk the come from his balls before they'd fully enjoyed their ride. He refused to shortchange either of them after anticipating this moment for nearly twelve months.

Shit, he'd been daydreaming about a twice-in-a-lifetime kind of love for a hell of a lot longer than that.

She felt amazing on his dick, smothering him and tugging at him in a way his fist could never imitate. Especially when she began to clutch the sheets in her hands and her heels drummed on the bed while her eyes rolled back a bit.

Tom had to abandon her mouth or risk getting bit when she thrashed her head from side to side. He dug his knees into the mattress and resisted the force she met him with as she bowed up, tensing every muscle he'd loosened, if only for a moment.

Her orgasm wrung his cock, making him freeze within her and concentrate on reciting the make, model, and year of every car he'd owned to distract himself from the temptation to spill deep within her. Not just yet.

Willie's eyes flew open and she collapsed onto his bed, barely able to suck in enough air to keep her from passing out for the second time that day, although obviously for a much better cause this time around. He smiled at her, wrecked and loose.

"That was...*incredible*," she said on an exhale that made her praise breathy and sexier than someone that worn out had a right to be.

"You mean *is*?" he asked, a wicked tilt to the corner of his mouth.

Willie wedged her hand between them, making him grunt

when she cupped her pussy and forked her fingers around his still-stiff cock, where it was clearly speared as deeply inside her as before. Rock hard, too.

"You didn't come?" she whispered, half in awe and maybe half in shock.

"Not yet." He shot her a smug grin.

"You weren't kidding about your expert-level prowess, were you?" Her lips formed a cute O as she realized he wasn't finished with her. Still. Hell, he was certain he would never get enough of this.

"Nope." He kissed her again, this time lingering while he flexed his hips a bit and got her used to the friction of his cock all over again. The veins on his shaft had to be bulging like those on a bodybuilder who'd taken far too many steroids at this point.

She didn't seem to mind.

"Tommy, I appreciate the thought, but I don't think—"

"Oh, no." He silenced her with yet another sweep of his mouth over hers. Then whispered, "You're coming with me. I'm not giving in to this alone."

"But you made me—"

"Yes, and you're far more brave than I could ever hope to be." He laid his forehead on hers and looked deep into her eyes. "Don't make me do this alone. I want you with me."

"I'll try," she murmured as she cupped the back of his head, rubbing her hand through his hair.

"Don't worry, I'll help." He gave her one last smacking buss then pushed upright so that he sat on his heels between her splayed legs.

"You're right." She swallowed hard as she watched him pull

out entirely then reintroduce his cock to her. Repeatedly. "That might do it."

"Oh, I haven't even gotten started with my assistance yet." He laughed, the sound strangled as he resisted his own mounting desire. There would be no constraining it this time.

A proficient lover, maybe. Superhuman, nope.

When he felt her melting around him again, he licked his thumb then laid his hand low on her abdomen so that his fingers splayed out over her and his thumb toyed with her clit. He leaned on her a little as he began to piston within her.

The headboard slapped the wall as he picked up steam, making him glad Quinn was safely out of the house again for the night. The ripple of her abdominal muscles against his palm had him grinning.

"Feel that, honey?" he hoped his question didn't sound quite so much like a snarl to her ears.

"It'd be pretty damn hard not to. You're not a small man, Tommy."

He laughed. "I meant the way your body responds to mine. We're made for this. For each other."

"Yes." She couldn't do much more than agree.

Tom thrust into her, torn between watching the affection in her stare, the bounce of her tits, and the disappearing act of his cock as her pussy gobbled him whole, over and over.

Yeah, that part definitely won out in the end.

He strummed her clit faster, in time to the shuttling of his hips, which fused them together tighter with each escalating impalement.

Willie didn't have to tell him she was close when she reached forward and dragged her nails down his torso from his chest to his abdomen, as if trying to cling to the moment. So he gave himself permission to unleash everything inside him, once and for all.

"Jesus!" he bellowed then fucked harder. "Take me, Willie. All of me. Fucking come on me and show me how much you love this. *Me.*"

If there was a hint of neediness to his command, he didn't mind. They had nothing to hide from each other anymore. As if she could tell how badly he needed her right then, her body answered his demand, peaking right when he thought he couldn't hold out another moment.

She came, drawing him with her into dazzling ecstasy.

Except as he poured himself deep inside her, it seemed that their rapture fed each other's. Every spurt of come that launched from his balls splattered against her flesh as if she was a canvas and he was painting a Pollock-esque masterpiece that would never be seen, only felt. Each blast seemed to trigger another clench of her pussy, stronger than the last.

He was almost afraid she'd squeeze his dick off with the violent chain reaction they caused when they mixed together like this. Still, he kept emptying himself into her until he was sure he couldn't possibly have anything left to give her.

Willie kept proving him wrong as she drew out his rapture along with his semen.

It felt unbelievable to flood her pussy, knowing there was nothing between them and never would be again.

"Mercy, Tommy," she panted. "Mercy."

He made some sound that was a quasi-laugh-meets-groan, withdrew from her pussy—which still contracted, if more softly—then collapsed on the bed beside her. He'd never been so drained.

The day and their lovemaking had sapped him of every bit of strength.

Willie picked up the slack for him, though. She tucked herself against his side then drew the covers up over them before patting his chest as if he was a prized thoroughbred instead of an exhausted and incredibly sated man.

"Son of a bitch," he muttered. "Either I forgot how damn good it is to fuck, or it's never quite been like that before."

"I know which it is for me." She smiled slyly up at him.

They angled their faces toward each other for one final drugging kiss. Tom wanted to tell her again how much he loved her. Some sliver of him didn't want to pressure her in case she could give him her body yet not her heart.

Afraid of ruining the best night he'd had in many years, he kept quiet a little too long. By the time he'd found his courage and whispered, "I love you, Willie. So damn much," the only response he got was her soft, adorable snore.

⇶ELEVEN

Willie stood in front of the mirror, fussing with her dress so that the giant white bandage on her arm wasn't so visible. The kids didn't need to worry over a scratch when she was about to drop a bomb on them.

Tom had finished getting ready ages ago. He sat on the edge of the bed, his eyes tracking her every movement. It might have been disconcerting if she didn't welcome his companionship, especially considering the impossible discussion she was about to have.

"Maybe we should have a doctor look at that cut?" he asked. "I thought about taking you to the ER yesterday…"

"You made the right call coming back here. It would only have stressed me out more waking up in the hospital." She shrugged. "I've survived worse."

Like the damage Steven had done that no one could see.

Except maybe Tom.

He stood then and crossed to her, hugging her to his solid chest. It had been so long since she'd felt this connected to a peer, someone other than her children. "We'll get through this, Willie."

"I know." That didn't stop her from dreading it, though. "Let's get it done."

He held out his hand and she took it, squeezing his fingers as they went downstairs. Quinn sat at the table eating some sugary cereal one of the Hot Rods had probably caved and bought for him.

"Good morning." She crossed to him and gave him a hug when she caught his nervous glance. "What are you doing home?"

"Came to get my Fruit Smashes." He bit his lip. "And to see if you were okay."

"I will be." She nodded. "I need to share something with Nola and Amber first, then I'm going to make you a healthier lunch and we can talk more about it, okay?"

"You mean about their dad still being alive?"

The innocent question from his mouth startled her all over again and she squeaked.

Tom steadied her then asked, "How do *you* know about that?"

"I was there last night, remember?" Quinn looked at them as though it was obvious. "When Gavyn and Kaige told Amber and Nola."

The rush of terror and dread that flooded Willie went straight to her head, making it ache despite the medicine she'd already taken in anticipation of the horrific news she had to break.

"I've got to go—" She would have bolted for her girls if Tom hadn't still had his arm around her, restraining her.

"Hang on a minute, Willie," he crooned to her. Then he asked Quinn, "Everyone was there together?"

The kid nodded with his mouth so full he looked like a chipmunk.

"How'd they take it?" Willie wondered.

"It sucked. Lots of crying and stuff. The rest of the gang took turns talking to them. Then they got pretty pissed off. Amber even broke a glass. I didn't know she could throw that good. Mostly, I think they're worried about you." He shoveled in another spoonful of cereal while Buster McHightops tracked the motion of the spoon from the bowl to his favorite kid's mouth then back, hoping for a dropped morsel.

"Maybe we'll have to put together a Hot Rods softball game, huh?" Tom grinned, ruffling Quinn's hair.

"Only if I get to be on her team." He smiled back weakly.

"Everything's going to be okay," Tom promised.

Willie wished she could believe it.

Quinn nodded and they headed outside, practically jogging across the lot to the Hot Rods' apartment. Before they'd even gotten halfway up the stairs, Amber opened the door and called out, "Momma!"

She rushed the rest of the way and flung her arms around her daughter, hugging her tight. It wasn't often the older of her girls broke down, or admitted she needed help, so it bruised Willie's heart even more when she felt the heaving of Amber's back as she sobbed quietly.

"Come on. Let's go in." Tom nudged them away from the stairs and shut the door behind them. No sooner had they made it into the Hot Rods' lair than Nola joined them in a three-way hug.

"It's really true, Momma?" she asked.

"Yes." She'd thought long and hard about what to say to her girls and she wanted to get it right. "Your daddy is still alive. He made some terrible decisions, but these should be happy tears."

"What?" Amber reared back. "You're not going to run back to him just like that, are you? He left us! I remember how many times there was nothing to eat or we were freezing in the car and you told us it would be okay because Daddy was watching over us from heaven."

Nola jumped in on that thought. "Fuck that, he was probably watching TV in his own comfy house. That bastard! How could he do that to us? To you? I know you would try to hold it in until we were asleep, but how many nights did we listen to you crying? Because of him!"

Willie looked to Tom, who nodded. She swallowed the bitterness that could poison her if she wasn't careful, then faced her daughters and said, "I'm not excusing what was done. However, I can forgive him. No, there's no future for Steven and me. Not even a chance. But I don't believe that being hateful is going to get us anywhere better than we've gotten ourselves already through caring for each other."

Tom hugged her tight.

Amber and Nola stared at her, their mouths hanging open as Gavyn and Kaige came to stand nearby, watching their backs. That's what was most important.

"Someday, when we're thinking more rationally, we could consider speaking with him. There might be some value in you girls having a relationship with him if he really has evolved. Or even if he hasn't. He's still your father."

"But he's not our dad." Nola crossed her arms and looked directly at Tom.

He rubbed his chest over his heart then gathered Nola to him in the crook of the arm not already around Willie. "Nothing will change that, Nola."

Willie breathed deeply to keep from succumbing to more tears. She didn't feel as if Steven was worthy of a single one more from her.

Just then the door opened and Quinn stuck his head in. "Hey, Willie. Can I butt in for a second?"

"Of course, come here." She motioned to the young man. "It's okay."

"Uh, there was a call for you at Tom's house. From…" He peeked at the note he'd scribbled on his napkin. "Dr. Smith's office. They said they've been trying to reach you, but you're not answering your cell. Tom was the emergency contact on file. They need you to call them back. Here. This is the number."

Willie accepted the crumpled, food-coloring-dotted paper with numb hands. "Okay, I'll give them a ring when we're done here. Thank you."

"Ms. Brown?" He didn't budge.

"Hmm?"

"The lady said it's urgent. She was kind of mean about it. I think you should do it now." He bit his lip. "Sorry, I wouldn't have come over here if it didn't sound important."

Tom stared down at her and she smiled back, ignoring his unspoken questions.

"Can I borrow someone's phone for a second?" She realized hers was probably still somewhere on the floor of her living room, where she'd dropped it yesterday.

Tom had his out and in her hand before she'd finished asking. He rubbed the back of his neck, taking quick, shallow breaths. "What the hell is going on, Willie?"

"I'm sure it's nothing." She went onto her tiptoes to kiss his cheek. "Let me just go somewhere quiet for a second and sort it out."

Willie darted down the hallway to the bathroom and closed the door, ignoring the troubled glances her daughters exchanged as she rushed past. Her fingers shook as she punched in the number Quinn had delivered then connected the line.

She knew it was probably not a good sign when it went to the triage station instead of the front desk at the doctor's office. "Hello, I'm Wilhelmina Brown. I was in for a scan a few days ago and—"

"Oh, thank goodness. We've been trying to get ahold of you." The woman did nothing to alleviate the nerves fluttering in Willie's gut. "There was an unusual shadow on your scans. We're going to need you to come back in for more detailed tests."

"Honestly, I'm having a terrible day. Family emergency." She didn't even know how to explain everything that had happened. "I feel much better now that I'm taking the medicine Dr. Smith prescribed."

"Ms. Brown, I don't mean to scare you, but I'm not sure you're grasping the severity of the situation. This isn't the sort of thing you want to play around with. We're talking about possibilities like an aneurysm, a hematoma, or…maybe…even a brain tumor. Can you come right now? I'd be glad to dispatch an ambulance for you if you need a ride."

She plopped onto the lid of the closed toilet.

"Are you joking?" They said the universe only dished out as much as you could handle. At this point it must think Willie was some kind of superhero.

"I'm sorry, ma'am. I wish I was."

"O-okay." A jolt of pain chose right then to flare in her skull. This time, it terrified her. She took a deep breath then waited, half-expecting to drop dead. "No need for the ambulance though. I'll get myself there."

"Soon?"

"I can be there in fifteen minutes."

"Great, I'll let them know you're on your way." The woman's voice softened when she murmured, "Good luck."

Willie splashed some cool water on her face then dabbed it off with the hand towel next to the sink. Then she stood there, staring into the mirror, attempting to perfect a natural-looking smile. When she got something as close as she could manage, she left the bathroom and prepared to give the performance of a lifetime.

How could she have been so selfish?

Sleeping with Tom to comfort herself when she'd known they were checking her out? It was reckless and irresponsible. After last night, they were *this* close to being permanently bonded. Repaying him for his endless kindnesses by making him relive his own worst nightmare was cruel and unusual punishment.

Willie refused to hurt him like that.

Overly chipper, she announced, "Looks like there was some

mix-up. They need to redo the scan they did the other day. Will you girls be okay if I take care of this quick? I'll come back as soon as I can and we can finish our discussion."

"Of course, Momma," Nola said though she squinted her eyes. She had a pretty honed bullshit detector. Probably too good for Willie's liking at the moment.

"At the same medical center on Broad?" Tom pinched the skin of his throat, his foot tapping manically on the textured concrete floor. "Go grab your purse. I'll get the car and pull around out front."

"It's not that big of a deal, Tommy." The wattage of her smile dialed up as if that would make it true. "You stay here and take care of that broken paver you were going to work on yesterday in the garden."

"Willie…" He flinched as if she'd struck him. "What's going on? If we're going to be partners in this thing—"

At least he hadn't called her his girlfriend.

"I'm sorry, Tom." She shrugged his warm, gentle hand off of her shoulder before it could erode her determination then lowered her voice, as if that would make what she was about to say private. "I don't think this is the right time to start something when there's so much happening at once."

"What?" He recoiled as if she'd burned him. "What the hell was last night? Seemed like more than a *start*."

"It was a mistake. I really am sorry. I shouldn't have. *We* shouldn't have—" She couldn't bear to finish that sentence. It was the worst lie she'd ever told, not to mention that the Hot Rods were mulling around, pretending not to hear the resounding implosion of their relationship.

"We can discuss it in the car. I'm still driving you downtown, even if you never want to sleep with me again." He headed for the door.

She stopped him with the coldest tone she could muster.

"I'm going alone. I don't need anyone to fight my battles anymore. I thought you understood that." Willie added a hand to her hip as she barged past him, out the door before he could follow. "Goodbye, Tommy."

Her heart caved in, crumpling into a decent imitation of a crushed soda can as it rattled around in her chest while she jogged to the parking lot. The whole time, she tried to erase the devastation in Tom London's gorgeous blue eyes from her memory.

There was no hope of that.

Only the fact that she'd hurt him some now, but less than if he had to watch her wither away, or die in his arms if her brain exploded after one too many stellar orgasms, could salve her conscience.

⫶TWELVE

Tom crouched in his garden gripping a rubber mallet so hard he was afraid the handle might splinter in his grasp. He took out his frustration on the thick stone he'd set into place, smashing it again and again. Even after it had leveled out with the path, he gave it a half dozen more whacks that sunk it far too low and cracked it in half. It broke worse than the hairline fracture of the original slab he was replacing.

"Fuck!" He tossed the mallet halfway across the garden then fell onto his ass. Bracing his elbows on his knees, he put his head in his hands.

He wasn't sure how long he stayed like that, trying to get himself under control.

"Tom?" a soft voice with a hint of an Asian accent called hesitantly. "Are you out here?"

For the first time in his life, he wanted to ignore one of his kids. He didn't. "Yeah, Sabra."

"Oh!" She nearly tripped over him before she realized he was tucked into the random outcropping of hostas.

He didn't lift his head, staring through his sunglasses at the assortment of shoes following hers. Looked like the lady Hot Rods were ganging up on him. Fan-fucking-tastic.

As if it were normal to have a powwow in the mulch, Mustang Sally approached and sat cross-legged next to him, her pink boots tucked under the legs of her coveralls. Sabra—a yoga expert—had no problem contorting herself into a spot between two of his plants. Even Kaelyn, somewhat prissier by nature, tucked her legs to the side and perched in the grass right outside the flowerbed. The three of them left room directly in front of him for Amber and Nola to join them, side by side.

"We thought we should come check on you." Nola broke their silence.

"What do you want me to say?" He shrugged. "That I'm fine? 'Cause, guess what? I'm not."

Kaelyn gasped.

It was impossible for him to muster an iota of optimism at the moment, despite more than a decade of insisting on it from his gang of misfits. "I gave it everything I had. There's nothing left. If that's not enough to convince Willie to quit running, then I'm out of ideas. And luck. Never had much of that anyway."

Thunder rumbled in the distance. Must have been from the black cloud hanging over him, he thought.

Sabra reached out and put her hand on his where it dangled, palm up, on his knee. He pulled away, ignoring the fist she pressed to her lips after he retreated from her touch.

"This isn't you, Tom," Sally scolded. "Since when are you a lame-ass quitter?"

"Since right about the time I finally thought Willie and I were on the same page only to hear her tell me she's not interested. A man can only take so much, you know?" He tried to breathe through the stabbing in his guts at that.

He'd been sure, when he fell asleep last night, that they were a couple. One that could go the distance.

Maybe he should have stopped with his massage. It seemed obvious now that she'd only turned to him because of the emotional fallout of confronting her husband. By taking her up on her offer at exactly the wrong time, he'd pushed her away.

"Hang on, I didn't hear her say she doesn't want you," Nola pointed out.

"I took it more as she's overwhelmed," Kaelyn added. "Understandable isn't it, given the situation?"

"Splitting hairs. Doesn't matter if she won't take me, or lean on me when things are tough. All it does is piss me off that things are broken and I can't fix them. On top of the other mountain of shit in her life, now I'm one of the screwed-up parts. The best thing I can do is leave her the fuck alone." Tom shrugged. "Look, I know you girls mean well, but how many times do I have to bang my head against the wall before I admit things aren't going to work out between Willie and me?"

He swallowed, ignoring the way Kaelyn gave her head a slow, disbelieving shake.

"Something's not right," Nola insisted.

Amber agreed. "I know my momma. There's no way she would lead you on like that then cut you out of her life. She's loyal, and careful to consider the people around her since she's been disregarded so many times in the past. Even if something had changed her mind about where things were going, she'd never have broken the news like that. It was crude, harsh, and... really indiscreet."

Tom tried to think about things. He couldn't quite see them from Amber's perspective, but it still didn't make any sense. So why had Willie shoved him away?

Maybe he had it backwards. He'd been a good fuck. What if that *wasn't* the problem? That didn't mean she'd gotten over the doubts Steven had instilled in her about trusting a man. How could she think Tom would let her down though? Had she cut off his chance to disappoint her by rejecting his concern?

Too many possibilities—every last one convoluted enough to make his head spin on a good day, which this one certainly was not.

"Tom, this whole situation is really screwed up. You're not seeing things clearly. What Momma did up there was shitty. Seriously. The only reasons I can think of she'd do something like that are terrible ones. I understand that you're knotted up over this, but I think—with whatever the hell is going on—she needs you now more than ever. Don't let her trick you into thinking otherwise. There haven't been many people who didn't bail on her. Except for Nola and me. That's different, though. Fight." Amber shook his forearm. "Please. Go find her. Given everything that happened yesterday, and now this, I'm scared for her. She'll talk to you straighter than she would us. See what the hell is wrong and take care of it, like you have for everyone else?"

"I told you, there are some things I can't fix, Amber. Besides, Willie doesn't want my help. She was very clear about that. I'm not the kind of asshole who disregards a woman's wishes or thinks she's not strong enough to handle things on her own when she plainly states otherwise." He ripped up a handful of grass then proceeded to tear it into green confetti, staining his scabbed knuckles.

"That's what she said, but I don't believe that's what she meant." Sally sniffled as she looked at Tom. "Remember when I left Hot Rods for a while? I told myself I might start over. I made the Powertools crew believe I could leave if I had to. Those were lies I was telling myself in case I had no choice. Building myself up so that I could try not to fall apart at the thought of life without Eli and Alanso. Plus the rest of these fools."

He couldn't ignore it when one of his kids hurt. "Ah, shit, Mustang. Come here."

She snuggled against his side and put her arms around his waist. "It's not fair, Tom. You deserve to be the happiest of us."

Nola and Amber looked at each other, engaging their sibling skills so they could have an entire conversation without words. At least it seemed that way. Finally, Amber nodded then looked toward Tom.

Encouraging her sister, Nola said, "He's what's best for her, Amber. It's not betraying Momma if it's for her own good. She'd say the same if she was making us take medicine we didn't like. Or pushing us into relationships we were afraid of."

"Okay." Amber frowned at Tom. "Why was it so easy for you to believe what was obviously a lie? Nola and I both knew as soon as it popped from her mouth."

"Huh?" Tom canted his head as he studied the sisters.

"Even I could tell, Tom," Kaelyn huffed. "When Ms. Brown came out of that bathroom, she was terrified. Freaking the hell out. No one is that still and that calm when they're breaking up with someone they're in love with, even if they think there's a valid reason to do it."

"What are you trying to say?" He scanned the five young women huddled around him, who glared at him as if he was a moron.

"Why would she hide the truth from you?" Amber wanted to know. "Unless…what if it's like you dreading telling her about Daddy? If you hadn't *had* to, would you have?"

"Son of a bitch!" Tom bolted to his feet, knocking Sally off balance. His eyes widened. They couldn't be right, could they?

"Momma was protecting him," Amber and Nola said in unison.

"It must be a hell of a lot worse than she was letting on." The air whooshed from him for a whole different reason this time. Tom bent in half, bracing his hands on his knees.

He drew in several ragged breaths before lifting his head to meet their stares.

Nola and Amber held hands.

"She knew you'd be paranoid about losing her like Michelle," Sabra whispered, horrified.

"Or maybe it's…" Sally looked at Nola and Amber, as if afraid to finish her thought. They all knew what she was thinking. Could it be too late already? Had the doctor called to give her the same terrible prognosis Michelle had gotten that February so long ago?

Tom couldn't stand the thought that something might be about to take Willie away from him so irrevocably. He knew too well there were no second chances and definitely no do-overs when you were playing with death.

"Let's go." Nola stood up, pulling Amber with her.

"Wait," Tom scrunched his eyes closed, trying to take everything in.

Things fell into place for him. The headaches, the medicine she'd started taking, maybe even how she'd passed out yesterday. He should have seen it. Should have realized she would downplay her ailment.

The way she'd tried to separate them earlier had been part of the act.

He'd been so wrapped up in making sure she survived her shock over Steven that he'd dismissed the main problem as symptoms of another crisis entirely.

If it hadn't been for everything with her husband, he would never have missed it.

Another reason to despise the man.

"Damn it!" He punched the side of his leg. "I think you're right."

"Tom, call us as soon as you know anything. Please!" Amber shouted to him as he ran, picking up steam.

"I will. Promise." When he got out to the lot, he realized his car was missing. Shit. Willie's was at her house from the day before. It must have been serious if she borrowed his without a word, not that he minded.

Tom sprinted to the Hot Rods garage.

"I need somebody's keys. Now!" He roared loud enough to be heard over the whir of pneumatic tools.

Alanso popped up from where he leaned over the engine of a gorgeous 1969 Firebird, so fast he banged his bald head then stood there rubbing it while cursing in Spanish.

Rolling from beneath another vehicle on their creepers, Kaige and Bryce stared at him as if he'd lost his mind. He was about to if someone didn't do as he'd asked.

Holden peered at him from where he upgraded the interior of a 500XL Ford Fairlane.

"Have you been drinking?" Roman asked when he and Carver looked up from their floor-standing toolboxes, where they'd been rummaging around for something or other. "You're not driving if you have."

"Fuck. No." He scrubbed his hands through his hair, trying to tame the wildness in him. If he had to run to Middletown, he would. When had his kids become such irritating, pain-in-the-ass, responsible adults, anyway? "I need to go after Willie, and she took my damn car."

"Well, why didn't you say so instead of coming over here looking all *loco*?" Alanso dug in his pocket and tossed Tom the key to his crotch rocket. That would work nicely.

He jogged to the bike and swung his leg over it, appreciating the sleek, bright-orange Honda REPSOL 600 even if it had a giant #69 decal on the side and was probably twenty times too flashy for a guy his age.

It was also ridiculously fast.

≋THIRTEEN

The Hot Rods T-shirt Tom proudly wore flapped in the wind as if it were a flag. He hunkered lower on the bike, leaning into it as he sped down the road.

Concentrating on his driving distracted him from terrible thoughts of Willie's fate.

Still, when he parked the bike near the main door to the medical center, a million different things ran through his mind. How he'd come to appointments with Michelle, held her hand when they told her there was nothing more they could do, left without her after she'd slipped away—he and Eli returning to their still, dark house by themselves.

It was difficult for him to even go inside. For Willie, he would.

Like he had for Roman last year after he'd nearly overdosed, Tom could smother his own panic if his relatives needed him.

Willie might not be blood. She was still family, and he wasn't about to let her convince him of anything else.

Wounded pride had nearly let her get away with deceiving him. She'd played off his insecurities. Never again would he allow his doubts to make him an easy target.

Steeling his spine, he concentrated on the only important thing here. Willie.

He dashed into the facility and checked the directory to make sure nothing had changed. It hadn't. He remembered the scans Michelle had gotten, the ones that showed more and more of the cancer eating her alive each time they'd bothered, until the doctors had given up.

Swallowing bile, he lengthened his strides, tearing up the linoleum floor as he blinked against the lights, harsh even with his sunglasses still in place. When he got to the desk, there was no one around.

So he marched to the door. He didn't give a shit about protocol.

If Willie was back there, he was going to find her.

Or he might have, if it hadn't been locked.

A couple bangs on the door didn't grab anyone's attention so he cursed then kicked the damn thing. While thinking about what to do next, seeing as Willie still didn't have her cell on her, and might not be able to answer in any case, the door opened and a man in a lab coat left.

Tom grinned and slipped in right behind the guy, who hadn't even noticed him.

There was a hallway with a bunch of doors on either side of it. Some of them were open, giving him a glimpse at the changing and prep rooms. Some were closed. He rifled through the charts hanging in the clear plastic bins outside two of them, dismissing those when he didn't see Willie's name.

Impatient, he resorted to more direct methods.

"Willie!" he bellowed. "Willie Brown!"

"Sir, you can't be out here." A stern-looking nurse with over-plucked brows and pursed lips headed in his direction, closing in quick.

Conjuring some believable story, other than *I'm trying to hunt down a patient who doesn't want me involved in her treatment*, he prepared to get booted out on his ass, or worse.

The nurse got within fifteen feet before a door, several down the hall, cracked open and Willie popped her head out. "Tommy! What are you doing causing a ruckus out there?"

He tossed the nurse a finger wave and muttered, "Got lost, sorry."

A massive frown coupled with a glare ensured she didn't believe him, but she let it slide when Willie made apologies and waved frantically for him to get inside her holding tank.

Fine by him.

"Have you gone bonkers?" Willie stood with her hands on her hips, looking every bit as hale and hearty as she had when she'd been meeting him thrust for thrust the night before.

"Only for you."

"Sweet talking will not get you out of this." She slapped her hand on his chest when he intentionally invaded her personal space. "Neither will kisses. Stop. Right. There."

"Why, Willie?" His jaw clenched.

Refusing to meet his stare, she studied the ugly hospital gown she had on instead. "Because. If you don't, I'm not going to be able to send you away again. This is no place for you."

Score one for the girls.

"Anywhere you are is where I want to be." He corrected her misguided thinking. Incredibly slowly, as if approaching a wild animal, he inched closer, his hands held out to her. "It's your headaches, isn't it? Something's really wrong."

Willie bit her lip, then nodded.

"Why don't you let me hold you for a minute?" he asked, still gently. "You're shivering. Pretend it's to get warm if you want."

Expecting her to decline, Tom got the wind knocked out of him when she flew to him and suffocated him with the tight grasp of her arms around his ribs. He hugged her back, rubbing his hands up and down her back to infuse as much warmth and reassurance as he could muster into her, given that his guts had frozen solid when she'd confirmed her health was poor.

"I'm going to talk for a bit. Just listen. And when I'm done you can decide what you want me to do. I'll go along with it, whatever you pick. Okay?" He nuzzled the side of her face as he spoke low and calmly into her ear.

She nodded against his shoulder.

"I think you blew me off this morning because you found out you're sick. Maybe really sick. I'm terrified. For you and for myself. For the girls, too. By the way, they were not fooled by your acting, though I was for a while. Nothing could be worse than being in the dark about what's happening. If you're not ready to talk about it yet—"

"I don't know what's wrong," she admitted.

"I thought I was going to talk to you." He smiled despite the situation. "Should have realized that was a silly plan."

Willie looked up at him and broke his heart all over again with a watery smile. "Sorry. For everything. How I treated you earlier…it was reprehensible. I hate myself. For that and for getting serious with you last night knowing there could be something wrong with me, even though I never imagined there actually was. It was just supposed to be a precaution when they did the scan the other day. I swear, I never would have done that to you on purpose. Not knowing everything. What you went through with Michelle, I mean."

She was critically ill and she was worried about was him?

If that wasn't love, he didn't know what was.

For now, that would be enough.

"Willie, if you think that I didn't love you because I hadn't put my cock inside you yet, then you really do have something wrong with your head." He wiped a tear from her cheek with his thumb then leaned in to give her a brief kiss.

She didn't turn away or push him back.

"Oh, whoops, I can come back if you need time to sort out personal matters…"

From the way Willie jumped in his hold, she hadn't heard the door open either.

"No, please." She slithered from his grasp, took a few steps, and held her hand out to the nurse, who'd already turned around. "I'd like to get the last of these tests over with if you don't mind."

That last bit she said while looking up at Tom.

"I'll be right outside whenever you're ready, Ms. Brown." The door closed with a quiet click.

Tom nodded when she peeked over her shoulder at him. "Whatever you need, Willie. I'll be waiting when you get back, okay? We can figure the rest out then."

"Thank you," she said then sniffled, her back to him once more. "I don't deserve you."

"No, you deserve a hell of a lot more." He rushed to her side, turned her around and laid a proper kiss on her lips then patted her ass through the gown. In his experience, the last thing a truly sick person wanted was to be treated differently than when they'd been well. "Go on. Be a good girl and maybe I'll give you a lollipop to suck on later."

"Tommy!" She may have sounded outraged, but she was smiling when she left him.

Tom sat in the crappy chair, only one step up from one of those metal folding kinds, for as long as he could stand it. Okay, so that was only like five minutes. Long enough for him to text Nola and tell her what little he knew. Mostly that he'd found Willie and she was having tests done.

Then he roamed the room reading every overly cheerful informational bulletin in the damn place. Everything from reminders to get an annual mammogram to diagrams of anatomical cross-sections to a description of neurological terms.

He focused on the ones that seemed relevant.

Aneurysm.

Subdural hematoma.

Intracranial pressure.

Brain tumor.

Wow, that had been a terrible idea. Except that he needed to be informed. For Willie's sake. Last go around there had been so many things he didn't understand, couldn't process. He would do better if he had to now. By the time he'd paced the room—which had more in common with a jail cell than a waiting area—enough to have walked to his nephew Joe's house a few states away, he'd started to tug on his hair. The motion made the strands stick out in weird ways that were exaggerated by the distorted reflection he kept catching sight of in the shiny metal canister that sat on the counter in the room.

He glanced at his watch. It had only been about forty-five minutes.

It seemed like a lifetime, especially when he didn't even know what specifically they were looking for. Reaching behind him, he rubbed his neck.

And that's when he heard Willie's voice coming back to him, along with the nurse's. The walls, though thin, garbled their discussions, keeping him in suspense. She sounded calm, though he'd only heard her lose it once. The day before.

When she came into the room, she crossed over to him and held his hand in hers. She was freezing, so he tried to rub some warmth into her fingers while she smiled softly up at him.

"They're going to admit me for observation while we're waiting for someone to read the tests," she told him. "If you don't want to stay, especially in the hospital section—"

"I'm going where you're going." There was no question about it.

"Okay, folks. Let's go." A nurse helped Willie into a wheelchair. The sight had his chest constricting.

"I can push her," he offered.

"Don't tell my boss." The nurse nodded and led the way.

It took a while to get settled, every second testing his patience anew.

When they were alone, or as alone as they would be in the hospital, he asked, "What are we looking at here, Willie?"

"They're trying to rule out an aneurysm and any kind of clot or bleeding on the brain." She sighed. "I'm not sure what I'm hoping for, but if it's not that then it could be…"

"A brain tumor," he finished for her.

Willie nodded. "Something is increasing the pressure inside my skull. They may have to do a procedure to drain fluid if my vision gets worse or they detect a big enough change from the scan they did the other day. They also did a bunch of blood work and other labs to see if they can detect any signs of cancer."

Her eyes closed when she said the c-word.

For his benefit more than her own, he was sure.

"Honey, it's okay." He clasped her hand in both of his. "I can handle this."

I think.

For you.

"I wasn't hoping for a relationship with you only when everything was going great or when both of us were doing fine. If you're sick, I'll take care of you. Like you would do for me. What I feel for you isn't conditional." He promised, "Whatever happens, we'll handle it together."

Willie opened her mouth a few times, like she wanted to say more. In the end she settled for a tiny nod. "Can you do me a favor?"

Tom's smile grew ten sizes. That she would even ask was progress. "Sure."

"Call the girls. If they want to come down here, I'd like to have them with me." She swallowed. "You're right. It's better to keep the people you love close."

Though she still didn't speak the three tiny words he craved, Tom knew she meant him, too.

If she couldn't say it now—wouldn't—because of her fears for the future, it was okay. He didn't need the verbalization to know it was true.

Almost the entire day had passed with hardly any updates. Tom grew restless as Willie's anxiety built. He got the nurses to administer her medicine, which they'd left at home, but even that didn't seem to help as the afternoon sunshine turned to twilight.

Despite her understandably elevated blood pressure and the increased stress of the day, Willie reported only a mild headache. After their earlier discussions, Tom actually believed her. A good sign, he hoped.

She looked over at her daughters. "Nola, maybe you should go on home. Ambrose—"

"Is fine. Kaige has her. She's got bottles prepared." Nola slouched, hunkering down instead of getting up to go. If her back and ass hurt even a fraction as much as Tom's did, he sympathized.

As Willie geared herself up to argue with her daughters, a doctor came into the room.

"Ms. Brown?" He held out his hand and shook Willie's slighter one.

"Nice to meet you."

"Likewise. I'm Dr. Rotman, your neurologist." He opened her chart then retrieved a printout and held it up. "This is the scan we took two days ago. This area here is where we're concentrating."

He gestured with the tip of his pen.

"Here's the scan of the same type we did earlier." He held up a second sheet of paper.

Tom though it was like watching static on an old, crappy

TV. He couldn't tell much, except maybe it looked less white. Was that good or bad?

"It appears the area of concern is changing."

"What does that mean?" she asked.

"Well, if it's a fluid buildup it could mean some of it is being absorbed by your body, which is great. It also helped us to rule out a few things. Combined with the other tests you have, we're confident you're not suffering from an aneurysm or a hematoma. That's a plus. Both of those are critical emergencies. What we're dealing with here is more stable."

Willie's gaze shot to Tom's. Brain tumor? *No.*

"If we find a mass in the final images that were taken from alternate angles, which take longer to analyze, or chemical proof of cancer in the labs, then we'll refer you to a specialist who can discuss your options for a more specific diagnosis." He cleared his throat then looked around the room. "However, what we hope we find, is nothing. No definitive answer."

"What?" Tom couldn't help himself from questioning the guy. Willie couldn't keep walking around with headaches, blacking out now and then.

"There's a possibility, though I don't want to get your hopes up, that this could resolve itself on its own." He shrugged. "There's a condition called pseudotumor cerebri. Frankly, we don't know what causes it, though it occurs most often in women between thirty and fifty. For some reason, our bodies can overproduce intracranial fluid. The increased pressure results in the same symptoms as a legit brain tumor. The drain you were informed about before would be one treatment, or, it could disappear gradually on its own."

"Those are a lot of *ifs*..." Willie's defeated tone had Tom squeezing her hand.

"Yes." The doctor didn't deny it. "Until we get the results of the rest of the tests, there's nothing more we can do for you." He tapped the foot of her bed twice with his pen.

"So she can leave?" It surprised Tom, given how dire things had looked that morning.

"The reality is, it's either going to be good news or bad news. Not much in between."

Nola and Amber looked about as ill as he felt at that declaration.

Willie peeked at them then shrugged. "Well, crap. What can you do?"

"I'm going to have the nurses discharge you so you can go home and get a good night's rest. Nothing much better than sleep for your body."

Tom could think of one thing that was.

"All you can do now is wait. I know it's not easy, but the advice I give my patients is to try not to think about it if you can. Terrorizing yourselves will not change the outcome." He looked around the room. "It looks like you've got the most important things already. Take advantage."

"I plan to." She tapped her finger on her lush lips. "So, there are no restrictions on what I can or can't do then, right?"

The doctor grinned. "Nope. I wouldn't recommend tackle football or anything like that, but..."

"How about a more relaxing full-contact sport?" Willie asked.

"Doctor approved." Dr. Rotman flashed them a thumbs-up.

"Momma!" Amber put her hand over her eyes.

Tom indulged her playfulness with a fist pump despite how raw his insides still felt.

"Tom! Gross!" Nola groaned.

"Payback, kids. It's a bitch." He winked.

Dr. Rotman grabbed his belly and boomed out a laugh at their antics. Then he said, "We'll call you tomorrow, as soon as we have more information. Of course, if any of your symptoms worsen, have one of these folks bring you back immediately."

As if Tom would take a chance with Willie's safety. "I'm on that."

"Good." Dr. Rotman squeezed Tom's shoulder then headed for the door. "It was a pleasure to meet you, Ms. Brown. I sincerely hope that I do not see you again tomorrow."

Willie giggled at that, making the doctor Tom's hero.

He quit fooling around since everyone—himself included—had been properly distracted, helping Willie sit on the edge of the hospital bed before gathering her clothes from the chair beside it.

"Hey, Amber?" Tom dug in his jeans pocket for Alanso's key. "Want to put that motorcycle license to good use?"

She'd recently gotten hers, claiming it was only fitting for a part-owner of Gavyn's sister-shop to Hot Rods, Hot Rides.

"Hell yes." She grinned.

"Oh, here we go. I'm never going to hear the end of how awesome this is." Nola rolled her eyes. "I'll see you at home."

"Not until tomorrow morning. Go play with that baby of yours and give her a kiss from Nana." Willie called to her daughters as they headed out, "Come for breakfast. Knock first."

"Momma!" This time Amber and Nola both shrieked it.

Earlier in the day Tom never would have imagined leaving this place laughing when everything still hung in the balance. Maybe he was a different man than he'd been thirteen years ago.

Instead of dreading the future, he wanted nothing more than to enjoy the now.

Especially if it was all they had.

FOURTEEN

They drove home in a companionable, if uneasy silence.

Sure, Willie was terrified. How could she be anything else?

If the worst happened, her daughters would go on without her. That didn't mean she didn't wish she could stick around to see them blossom beneath the love and attention their guys showered on them. Then there was baby Ambrose. Who would teach her how to sew or what the names of all the pink flowers were or bake cute birthday cakes for her each year?

That was supposed to be her job.

The injustice of it threatened to overwhelm her. Not only for herself, but also for the man beside her, who drove with one hand on the wheel, his fingers drumming madly, while he used the other to cradle her fingers as if they were the most precious things in the universe.

"What's that big sigh for?" he asked her.

"I'm still not sure I'm doing the right thing here," she admitted as they rolled into the Hot Rods lot. "For you, I mean."

"I'm a grown man. Let me worry about myself." He kissed her knuckles then came around to her side of the car. A gentleman spoiling her with politeness was a luxury she hadn't indulged in much since her youth. So she waited for him to open her door. Not because she couldn't do it herself, but because she appreciated the false sense of security it lent her at the moment—reassurance that he would take care of her if she let him.

Before she climbed the stairs and walked into his home again, she had to be absolutely sure that was okay with him since she couldn't imagine ever having the strength to peel her soul away from his if they linked any tighter.

Who was she kidding? It had nearly killed her to leave him in the apartment that morning. It was already too late.

"What if it's bad news?" she whispered to him.

"My heart will be broken." The raw agony in his bright eyes tore at her. "But Willie, if you leave me *now* that's guaranteed pain. So really, my odds are better with only the chance of getting hurt. And even that wouldn't happen for some unknown amount of time down the road."

When she thought about it like that, she figured she couldn't argue.

"We're not dumb kids anymore, honey. No matter what we do from here on out, one of us is going to go first. Hell, I'm kind of surprised I didn't stroke out last night when I came inside you." He put his hands on either side of him, opening his arms wide. "Nothing is guaranteed in life. Which is why I want *you* to be sure. Can you dedicate your time to something between us? Something real and lasting? For however long we might have? Tell me now if you can't, Willie. It's fucking with my head not knowing where I stand with you."

"The only thing I'm certain of right now is that no matter how much time I've got left—a minute or fifty years—I want to spend it with you, Tommy." She kissed him gently, though the brush of their lips quickly evolved into something a heck of a lot more sensual. "Does that clear it up?"

"That's good enough for me."

"Well, you heard the doctor." Her fingers flexed on his abdomen. "He told me to take advantage of you."

As she hoped, Tom laughed, full and loud. Like he had often before this week had tested them in every possible way. His eyes twinkled. "I'm pretty sure that's not what Dr. Rotman really meant, but I'm willing to go along with your intentional misinterpretation."

"That's very kind of you, sir." She poured her accent on thick.

"Have I ever told you how fucking hot that southern belle factor is?" he growled then hoisted her over his shoulder, palming her ass and trapping her knees to his abdomen as he sprinted inside.

Willie couldn't stop laughing, not even when he set her on the kitchen table then stepped between her knees. "I'll have to remember that."

"Then again, pretty much everything you do turns me on," he admitted when he buried his face in her cleavage. "Like these pretty dresses you wear. They've been teasing me by showing off your curves. I can't wait to get my hands on them again."

"What're you waiting for then?" She rocked from one side

183

to the other to lift the skirt of her dress from beneath her then pulled it over her head.

Tom took it from there, unhooking her bra by feel alone faster than she could have herself. He whisked it away then worked her panties off her legs. Before she knew it, she was perched on the kitchen table, entirely nude.

"You going to keep standing there licking your lips, or make a meal out of me, Tommy?" She couldn't help but tease him when he stared at her like a starving man about to feast.

"Tell me if it's too much." He paused. "If you start to feel unwell..."

"Not possible when I'm with you like this. Don't you dare be delicate with me now. I may be broken already. There's nothing you can do to damage me. Ever." She held her arms out to him.

Only leaving her hanging long enough to strip, Tom pounced, shoving her backward until she was spread out across the table for him to thoroughly enjoy. Suddenly she had a wicked inspiration.

"You never did eat that chocolate pie I made for you."

He blinked a few times. "That's not what I'm hungry for right now, Willie."

"Maybe I want some...licked off of you." Glad he wouldn't be able to see her blush, she added, "I've never fooled around like that before and I don't want to wait anymore to try everything I've ever dreamed about. I've got you and I've got a pie. Sounds like the perfect time to me. Bring it over here. Get me dirty, Tommy."

"I like it when you sass me, Ms. Brown." He lunged for the neatly covered dish on the counter then set it on the bench seat of the table, tearing into it.

Fear instilled some desperation in their lovemaking.

She found she enjoyed the edge it lent to her thrill.

Never before had she been able to fully let go and surrender to the moment without thoughts of what would come beyond the now. Today, that might be all they had.

It was freeing *and* terrifying.

Tom skipped utensils entirely. He gouged his fingers into the chocolate pudding and whipped topping she'd arranged in layers. Scooping the first dollop onto two fingers, he offered it to her. She ate it, greedily.

Before she could swallow the large helping he'd fed her, not so neatly, he swooped down for a kiss, licking the sweet cream he'd left on her lips. He moaned into her mouth as he tasted the combination of her and the confection she'd baked for him.

"I definitely like it better this way." He grabbed another blob, this time smearing it along her chin and down her neck. "You're brilliant…and delicious."

Laughter spilled from her as he tickled her with his mouth, then set her ablaze with its skilled attack. When he went to the pie again, he didn't mess around. Tom grabbed two handfuls of the filling then smooshed them onto her breasts.

The shock of the unwarmed confection was lessened by his mouth, cleaning her off again. He must have really liked it. He didn't leave a single morsel on her skin. "Tommy. My turn."

"No way. I'm not full yet." He grinned, chocolate smeared across his handsome face.

So she took matters into her own hands. Literally.

Willie spun around on the table, dipping into the pie herself before continuing her rotation until she sprawled on her back with her head near his body. Now she had a much better view.

Tom's cock hung thick and heavy right above her. She reached up and slathered him in pudding, loving the way his shaft twitched in her palm.

He hissed. "Fuck, that's kind of cold. You should have told me."

"Liked it." She didn't bother to argue, instead nibbling along his length then opening her mouth so he could feed her his delectable, chocolate-covered cock.

Tom groaned, flexing his hips a few times to give her more of himself. He left the pie to her, so she occasionally added more sweetness to his natural spice. Instead, he tipped forward, bending at the waist.

Bracketing her hips with his palms, he settled for a different sort of treat.

Willie moaned when his tongue flicked across her clit.

Wishing he had another hand to prop himself up so he could push a few of his thick fingers inside her, she groaned and walked her heels outward until they rested on the very edges of the table, giving him as much leeway as possible.

Pleasure built inside her rapidly, driven by the incessant massage of his mouth on her most sensitive bits. When she flew apart, the orgasm seemed brilliant but fleeting compared to those she'd achieved while he was buried balls-deep inside her the night before.

Dessert forgotten, she began to beg. "Fuck me, Tommy."

"No more waiting, Willie. Not tonight. Never again." He didn't disappoint. He collected her from the table, helping her cling to him so that her arms wrapped around his neck and her legs around his waist. The nudge of his cock against her pussy as he began to climb the stairs had her squirming.

"Whoa." He tipped forward a little, putting one hand on the stairs above her head as he steadied them.

Except the position had them aligned so perfectly that the tip of his cock prodded her entrance. "Right here, Tommy. Right now."

He seemed like he might argue. Instead, what came out of his mouth was, "What the fuck? Why not?"

His tight, high ass clenched, thrusting his cock forward and into her clinging sheath.

They both moaned at the reintroduction of his erection into her body.

He pushed into her more, but couldn't quite fit them together as well as she would like since she kept slipping without a good handhold.

"Hang on." No way could she go as far as the bedroom. She could make things easier on him, though.

A frustrated, impatient sound left his chest when she separated them. Only long enough to turn over. His hand steadied her, ready to catch her if she slipped as she got into position, kneeling on the stairs, bent forward, her forearms braced higher up.

The position shoved her ass out at Tom.

"Fuck, yes." He didn't ask for permission before he spanked her once, twice, then a third time, infusing heat and a rousing tingle in her cheeks.

Tom stood behind her, ringing the base of his shaft as he got situated, then sank into her pussy. She screamed, and he paused, just for a moment to let her adjust.

"No. Go. Fuck." She didn't care that her desperation was evident in the total shutdown of her mind. "Now, Tommy."

He put his hands on her waist, curling his fingers around to her belly while his thumbs rested at the top of her ass. Using the grip, he slid her back as he leaned forward then reversed their motions. He drove into her, harder and faster than he had dared the night before.

Willie locked her arms to hold herself steady, proving to them both that she was capable of accepting anything he could give her. Grant both of them, really, though sometimes loving this wildly could be terrifying.

Before long, rapture started to spiral higher in her. Her breasts rasped against the carpet of the stair treads and her knees had rug burn that would be hard to explain to the doctors. Taking control of her own ecstasy, she transferred her weight to one arm then slid the other one between her legs.

"God, yes." Tom pumped into her, reaching deeper with each stroke as his cock opened her up and eliminated the last of her resistance. "Rub your clit for me, Willie. Make yourself come on me. I love to watch you unravel."

It was an easy enough request to fulfill when he possessed her as if he never intended to stop or let her go. Thrilled to be alive and participating in this new, raw, exhilarating experience with the man she loved, she couldn't deny him her pleasure.

Willie's spine arched, her head snapped back, and Tom gave her the last push she needed to fly when he took one hand off her waist to wrap it in her hair and tug as he continued to fuck within her.

Her fingers flew over her clit, rubbing in her favorite pattern, one she'd discovered in the lonely nights she'd spent before meeting the sexy garage owner. She shattered, her pussy drawing at Tom's cock as if to keep him from retreating even a fraction of an inch as she pulsed around him.

Slowing though not stopping entirely, Tom rode out her climax. He kept her from collapsing or losing the spark of her arousal with his periodic thrusts.

When she felt need building inside her for more friction, more force, she whimpered.

"Shh, honey. I'll give you more." He wrapped his arms around her middle then lifted, climbing the rest of the stairs. His heavy erection slipped from her as he moved, making her moan at the loss.

Not for long though.

Because when they got to the top and only a few more feet down the hall, halfway to his bedroom, Tom cursed. "I have to have you."

He picked her up, facing him again, and she did what she could to facilitate as rapid a return of his cock to her pussy as possible. She locked her legs around his trim waist and hooked one heel over the ankle of her opposite leg.

With her weight resting on his hips, Tom concentrated on getting his thick hard-on back where it belonged. Inside her.

He reached down and guided himself to her clutches. They joined once more, both of them gasping at the delight. It surprised and surpassed memory each time. With that accomplished, Tom shifted his arms, putting his palms flat on the wall. His forearms absorbed the pressure of their mass as he fucked into her.

She put her hands on his shoulders and used him to push off of, allowing gravity to pull her onto him over and over. They fell into a rhythm that was faster, shallower, and more urgent than the pace they'd set previously. The change meant he never left her much, but when they came together it was as fully as possible.

Her clit knocked the pad of muscle above the base of his cock with every pass.

By grinding herself on him, she was able to find that seductive place where everything fled her mind and left only rapture instead of fear or worry. Why would she ever want to stop when it felt so good?

"That's right, Willie." He bit her lower lip, staring into her eyes for a while before kissing her ferociously. "Make me yours."

Only fair since she'd been his since about three seconds after they'd met a year ago.

His mouth slid over hers, eating at her as eagerly as he had the tastes of her ruined pie.

Their tongues speared between each other's lips, twirling around as he lapped up the frenzied sounds she made and surrendered some primal groans of his own. Each one spurred her on.

When their exertion made their skin slippery with light perspiration, she had a harder time keeping him right where it felt best. He switched his grip to her ass, holding her up as his shoulders pinned her to the wall. A groan of frustration turned instantly to one of satisfaction when the change in position made him far better able to deliver the full length of his cock to her pussy, plunging within her with slaps of his hips hard enough to knock a photograph off the wall beside them.

She would have laughed at their exuberance and impatience to have each other, except she was far too needy to find it amusing. The angle of his pelvis altered slightly as one or the other of them shifted in their precarious perch.

It made his blunt tip strike the wall of her pussy in precisely the right spot to steal her ability to resist a moment longer. Combined with the tap of his body on her clit and the adoration in his eyes as he ravaged her, she surrendered.

He didn't even wait for her to finish coming before he carried her the rest of the way into the bedroom. Each of his footsteps caused another burst of ecstasy to overwhelm her, extending her orgasm.

Still connected, Tom tumbled them to the bed, where they bounced and crashed together some. Unwilling to lock away the inhibition-less vixen he'd unleashed, she kept rolling until she was straddling him, shoving his shoulders into the mattress as she shot him a wicked smile.

"Oomph," he groaned. "Willie, I won't be able to last much longer if you ride me."

The thought of putting cracks in his shell of control thrilled her. To know she could was amazing. A man like him at her mercy...the thought boggled her mind and drowned it in arousal.

"You're so fucking beautiful." He watched her as though he admired the strength, grace, and abandon she possessed when she was with him like this. He brought out the warrior in her and they both enjoyed the results.

Even a week ago, she might have worried about the sway of her heavy breasts, which hung much lower than they used to, or the full curve of her belly. Now, she didn't think of anything except how wonderful it was to partner with him on generating as much rapture as possible for them both to share.

His cock filled her to capacity in this position, driving inside her so that his head tucked against the far reaches of her body. It would have been impossible to take him deeper, yet she felt like this time, when they stared into each other's eyes without blinking, he'd traveled much further—all the way to her soul.

She lifted a hand to caress his cheek gently, letting her index finger dip into his mouth. He sucked on it lightly, nipping the tip only when she lingered.

Willie put her hands on his chest, letting him support her weight—he could handle it—while her thumbs brushed over the hard discs of his nipples.

When he began fucking into her from below, she knew he was close.

"Are you going to flood me, Tommy?" she asked. "Let me feel how much you want me. How much you love me, because I know it's not even a fraction of what I feel for you."

She ground onto him as he roared, the tendons in his neck standing out as he walked the razor's edge. Knowing exactly how to tempt him into joining her, her pussy already starting to clench around his fat girth, she stared into his eyes and finally told him the absolute truth.

"I love you, Tommy. Always will."

His fingers clenched on her ass, digging in, though she didn't mind. The eight points of pain heightened her own release. Not as much as the warm blasts of his come inside her did though. Feeling his heat and lust in such an undeniable demonstration of how she affected him would never fail to impact her.

Their pleasure spiraled higher. Each pulse lifting each other to the next peak as their joy expanded exponentially, their love for each other acting as a bonus multiplier, making both of them winners.

This time they stayed joined after he finished emptying himself inside her.

Willie took his face between her hands, brushing the corners of his mouth with her thumbs as she smiled down at him. "Tom London, my Tommy..."

"Mmm." His smile was gigantic and illuminated her entire world, even if it was a little self-satisfied and goofy in the aftermath of their feral romp. "Tell me again."

"I just thought you should know how very much I love you. No matter what happens tomorrow. Or the next day. Or ten years from now...I always will."

Relief erased subtle lines from his face, making her realize that she was seeing him fully content for the first time ever. Withholding that information under the guise of doing it for his own good had been exactly the wrong choice.

She would never make that mistake again.

"I love you too, Willie." He kissed the tip of her nose. "I thought I couldn't possibly love you more than I did before. Then you went and unleashed your inner sex-starved wildcat. Holy shit. She's my favorite side of you yet."

"I'm glad, because I think you'll be seeing a lot more of her in the future." She propped herself up on his chest so she could see him better, staring adoringly into his eyes until they began to droop. Then she kissed him sweetly and snuggled down into his hold, knowing he wouldn't let anything bad happen to her.

At least not tonight.

And not if it was in his control.

The rest…well, that was up to fate.

Willie counted her blessings like sheep as she dozed off, thinking of how they outweighed the negative aspects of her existence. If that was all she would have in her lifetime, she couldn't complain. Accepting whatever news tomorrow would bring might not be easy, but she was determined to do so with dignity and the help of those who loved her.

Something was buzzing.

Willie moaned in protest and tried to ignore it, so she could stay in her warm, comfortable nest with Tom. Unless he was waking her up with languorous morning sex, she wasn't interested in rousing.

Another insistent *rrrrrrr* refused to let her play dumb.

Tom beat her to fully awake. "It's your phone."

For a moment, he stared at the damn thing one of the kids had retrieved from her house. It vibrated on the bedside table as if it were a snake warning off a hiker that had wandered too close. Neither of them wanted to get bit.

Then he looked to her and asked, "Ready?"

"Answer it." She nodded.

Tom rolled onto his side, facing her, and she mirrored him. He dropped the phone between them then swiped accept and tapped the speakerphone icon.

"Good morning, Ms. Brown."

"I've got you on speaker, Dr. Rotman." She cleared her throat, wondering what to call Tom. Boyfriend sounded ridiculous for a man as developed as him. "My partner, Tom, is here, too."

"Great, I'll make this quick. Your labs came back negative— every one. The scans are clear as well." His cheerful voice made it obvious how glad he was to be able to ease their worry instead of handing out death sentences, as he sometimes must have to do.

Tom's exhale was strong enough to blow her hair in front of her eyes.

"Thank you," he murmured while looking upward, blinking several times in rapid succession.

Elation sang through her veins, making the rest of what the doctor was saying kind of blur together. All she could think was what a miracle it was that she'd been granted more time with Tom and the rest of her growing family.

"We're still going to need to follow up. Another image in forty-eight hours, then again in a week. If things stay as they are, the fluid will probably disappear on its own. If it needs some help, we'll perform a fairly minor procedure. Until then, your medicine should help control the symptoms. If not, please come in right away."

"I'll do that. Thank you so much."

"I'm always happy to make these kinds of calls. Stay well."

"You too," she said before they hung up.

"I guess Dr. Rotman was right," Willie teased. "Sex and sleep worked like a charm."

They both knew it was more serious than that, their near miss. They'd gotten lucky in life's game of Russian roulette this go around. They wouldn't always.

It helped to move on to the next moment and not dwell on the past, or pretend like they would dodge that bullet eternally.

Whatever challenges they faced on the—hopefully—long road ahead of them, they'd do it together without wasting a moment more than necessary worrying about the end.

Starting right then.

Willie pulled Tom on top of her, purring when his already hard cock nudged her clit.

Breakfast was going to be served a little late.

Oh well.

≡EPILOGUE

Quinn watched in awe as a freakishly fancy candle spun around on top of the cake Kaelyn had baked in honor of Tom's fiftieth birthday. She and Amber had organized a huge surprise party that even their friends, the Powertools crew, were attending from a couple states away.

The bumblebee Camaro SS replica candle looked exactly like the car the Hot Rods had restored as a gift for their dad. It was the first vehicle Tom had ever owned, with a few special modifications—of course—that they'd even let Quinn help with.

The toy version spun around with pre-recorded engine roars while shooting some serious fireworks out of its miniature mufflers while Tom grinned, pumping his fist.

Though it was seriously awesome, Quinn couldn't wait for Tom to blow it the hell out so they could get to the best thing of the day. Not the opening of Tom's other presents or even the part where they got to scarf delicious cake.

He kept bouncing on his toes, hardly able to keep the secret anymore. "Come on, Dad! Make your wish already!"

Tom looked up and shared a covert smile with Quinn as he blurted the line they'd practiced earlier that morning.

"It's hard to think of something I want." Tom surveyed the group of family and friends surrounding them. Eli, Alanso, and Sally stood by his side. Then Kaige and Nola, who held Ambrose, next to Amber and Gavyn, their hands linked. Bryce, Kaelyn, Sabra, and Holden were still staring at the car candle doing its thing. Roman and Carver were watching each other instead from where they stood with Quinn, who had Buster McHightops at his feet.

Joe, Tom's nephew, bounced his son Nathan in his arms, distracting him from wanting to play with the non-kid-safe toy. His wife Morgan and the rest of the Powertools crew huddled behind them. Then, immediately beside Tom, was Ms. Brown.

Tom turned to her as he said, "The only thing I could wish for is Ms. Brown."

She laughed at his antics. Then her nose wrinkled. "I'm not sure I want to be called that anymore, Tommy."

Quinn watched without blinking as Tom cupped her face gently in his hands and stole a quick yet tender kiss. When she sighed, he asked, "Would you prefer to be called Mrs. London instead?"

Her eyes opened wide and her whole face lit up brighter than the candle, which had fizzled out.

When she couldn't quite find the words to respond to Tom's question, he reached into the pocket of his jeans and took out the velvet box holding the ring he'd picked out with the help of his sons and future daughters-in-law, twice over.

Quinn glanced around at the Hot Rods, noticing several of them had tears running down their cheeks. It made him feel better about the stinging in his eyes.

Tom sank to one knee and took Willie's shaking hand in his. Her other one was pressed to her lips.

"Willie, I know it's been a long time coming, but this kind of happiness is worth the wait, however long. Now that we've found it, I don't ever want to let it go again." He kissed her knuckles then cracked open the box, showing her the dazzling ring inside.

The thing was ginormous.

Tom had said he wanted the biggest damn diamond they could find since Willie had never had one before. He wanted it to shine half as brightly as she did. Around the center stone and along the entire band, a rainbow of gems twinkled. They were the birthstones of all the Hot Rods and Powertools. They'd even included Amber, Gavyn, and Quinn.

He was the little blue part, right there next to his brother's green one.

The colors reminded Quinn of the rainbows that had appeared after the storm at the quadruple wedding earlier that year.

"Tommy!" she gasped.

"I love you, Willie. Will you marry me?" He held the ring out, clasped between his thumb and index finger. Then he kissed each of her fingers and aimed them toward the symbol of their love.

Quinn's heart was racing, although he knew there was no way she'd turn Tom down. Something inside him unknotted when it finally sank in that there were people in the world who were mostly decent instead of mostly bad, like his mom.

They cared about others and worked together for the greater good.

Even better yet, he could become one of them, too.

He couldn't wait for the day he met the person he was supposed to spend the rest of his life with, no matter how long it took to find her. Or him. Or them.

Roman looped his arm around Quinn's chest from behind instead of teasing him about his crying.

"Yes! Yes, of course!" Willie shrieked. "What are you waiting for, Tommy? Get that ring on my finger this instant."

He obliged her, then rose, bundling her in his arms as he laid a giant kiss on her lips.

In fact, he made out with her for so long, dipped over his arm, Quinn wondered how she didn't pass out from lack of air. When they finally seemed to remember they were surrounded by almost thirty people, they looked around with grins that would put the Joker to shame.

"Well, I realize it'll probably be anticlimactic after that," Nola teased. "But, speaking of names, I think it might be a good time to show you my gift, Tom. It's really for myself, too. All of us, I guess."

"Let's see it." He beamed, hugging Willie tight to him as if he might never let her go again.

Nola carefully handed Ambrose to Kaige then tugged on the V-neck of her shirt.

"Haven't we seen your boobs enough, lately?" Quinn groaned, considering how often she'd been breast feeding around the house.

Roman lightly smacked him upside the head, laughing as he did it. "Behave."

As everyone chuckled, Nola uncovered the site of her tattoo. The one of her dad's name—Steven.

Except it didn't look the same anymore.

"I had it covered up." She peeked at her mom, as if a little nervous. "I figured it was more important to wear the names of the parents who loved me enough to put up with me my whole life, instead of the one who'd bailed. Instead of missing what I didn't have, I should have appreciated what I've got. What we all have."

Quinn peeked through his fingers, gasping when he saw the tribute to Tom and Willie. Their names were tangled together inside a heart that was made up of two things. Half of the heart was a gas pump, the hose curving around then down to the point at the bottom. On the other side it was a needle with thread that mirrored it.

At the base, they twisted together, completely entangled.

Ah, shit. Quinn accepted the skull and flame handkerchief his brother handed him when he sniffed. This time, when he looked around, there wasn't a dry eye in the whole place. Even Mike, the foreman of the crew, let his daughter Abby—who he held—wipe away a tear from his cheek.

Tom and Ms. Brown—no, soon-to-be Mrs. London—fawned over the design for quite a while. As people began to head toward the couple to congratulate them with hugs and thrilled squeals, Willie got the final say. "I guess the Hot Rod doesn't fall far from the tree."

Tom's face whipped toward her as his brows shot up and he said, "You didn't!"

"I most certainly did." Willie pushed up the fluttery arm of her sundress—her ring nearly blinding Quinn as it reflected the sunlight on the roof deck—to reveal the Hot Rods logo, tattooed with awesome white highlights that stood out on her dark skin. It covered up the scar she'd gotten the day she found out Steven was alive. It was badass. He was *so* jealous.

"No fair! When can I get mine?" he asked as Tom inspected the brand that matched his own.

"When you're eighteen." A smile curved up Willie's lips as she promised him, "I'll take you myself."

"I'll come, too." Roman clapped him on his shoulder.

"You're going to need to find a pretty big shop so all of us can be there." Sabra winked at him. "I wouldn't miss it."

Quinn couldn't wait. He knew that although they'd had some adventures already, the best times were ahead of them. Gavyn was teaching him lots of stuff about motorcycles, including sneaking in a few lessons on how to ride them even though he was only fifteen. And they'd even been talking more about him visiting Bare Natural during the summer to spend some time with Nathan and Abby as they got bigger.

He had a feeling it wouldn't be long before there were more Hot Rod babies, too.

Pretty soon he was going to be the big brother of a whole new generation.

Wouldn't that be awesome?

THANKS FOR READING!

Did you enjoy this book? If so, please leave a review and tell your friends. Word of mouth and online reviews are immensely helpful to authors and greatly appreciated.

To keep up with all the latest news about Jayne's books, appearances, merchandise, release info, exclusive excerpts and more, sign up for her newsletter at **www.jaynerylon.com/ newsletter** More than 25 prizes are given out to subscribers in each monthly edition.

SHOP AT JAYNERYLON.COM

Check out Jayne's online shop for autographed print books, direct download ebooks, reading themed apparel, mugs, totes, notebooks, Mr. Rylon's Wood and more at:

www.jaynerylon.com/shop

SNEAK PEEK!
NIGHT IS DARKEST
MEN IN BLUE, BOOK 1

If you enjoyed the Hot Rods, and the related Powertools books, you may also like Jayne's sexy romantic suspense series, Men in Blue. Check out this group of hot cops and the women they fall in love with as they race to solve murders, shut down underground sex slavery rings, and destroy the formula to an illicit super-drug.

————

Some secrets refuse to stay hidden.

Lacey Daughtry's perfect weekend is interrupted by tragic news of her brother's murder in the line of duty. Plagued by a rash of mysterious phone calls, she turns to her brother's best friends and fellow officers for protection…and comfort.

Spending time in close contact with Mason and Tyler, the two men she's dreamed of since her first girlhood crush, seems like the answer to a prayer. Especially when they begin to explore the desire she's harbored for so long.

But the partners are holding out on Lacey. Determined to suppress the most extreme facets of their lust, they agree to settle for sharing the woman they crave while concealing their desire for each other. Until Lacey cracks their resolve, unleashing a torrent of emotions that threatens to distract them when they can least afford it.

1

Their blossoming relationship is complicated by secrets. And the only way to evade the killer threatening their lives is to bare their souls in the darkest hours of the night. Or everything will come crashing down, just before the dawn.

Warning: After reading this book you'll never look at a pair of hot cops, a cemetery or a can of Spaghetti-O's the same way again.

———

Schwullllmp.

L acey could guarantee that the eerie sound of the first shovelful of dirt landing on the polished surface of her brother's coffin would reverberate through her nightmares for eternity. The skittering of pebbles adding one more barrier between her and her last blood relative caused her to flinch. A warm, gloved hand reached out to bracket her elbow. Tyler. She didn't have to turn around to recognize his steady, comforting touch. He and Mason stood resolute behind her in their dress uniforms like her own personal honor guard.

Her spine straightened. She drew her shoulders back and lifted her chin against the agony she struggled to hold at bay. Rob would be proud of her stoic bearing. Though, in all honesty, she couldn't cry. She hadn't shed one single tear since she'd received the news of his ultimate sacrifice. Whoever he'd died to protect, she prayed they were safe. She had to believe his loss held some value.

With dry eyes, she scanned the monstrous crowd. Rows of black clad mourners, so deep she couldn't make out the end, ringed the gravesite beside her parents' under the oak tree in the city's oldest cemetery. The preacher's speech—designed to comfort—couldn't penetrate the gloom in her heart, which complemented the dreary, overcast day. In her mind, she heard Rob's laugh, then replayed the petty argument they'd had over dirty dishes last Wednesday, before remembering his daily warning.

"Stay safe." It was the last thing he'd ever said to her. He'd whispered the standard entreaty in her ear as he captured her in a bear hug before she'd headed off to work Friday evening. In her mind's eye, it seemed he held her tighter—for a moment longer—than usual, but she recognized the wishful thinking.

If only he'd listened to his own advice.

She shivered against the October breeze as crispy leaves wandered past the pointed tips of her black leather boots. A few moments later, Mason's jacket enveloped her. Lacey tugged the lapels over her breasts, soaking up the heat of his body. She could make three fitted coats from the fabric that had so recently framed his broad shoulders.

Over the past several days she had thrown herself into the preparations for this service and the party—she refused to call it a wake—that would follow. At no time had she been left alone. Though they'd stayed in touch with the fruitless investigation, one of Rob's best friends had accompanied her while she delivered Rob's dress uniform to the funeral home, selected music and readings, gave input into the obituary she'd penned and stopped just short of following her to the bathroom to see if she needed their assistance to wipe her ass.

They were driving her insane.

Mason nudged the base of her spine with a discreet pat. "Go ahead, doll. Do you need me to escort you?"

She blinked to clear the haze from her mind. The police commissioner now stood at the edge of the jagged hole in the ground, sparing her a glance drenched with pity. In his outstretched hand rested Rob's badge, hat and service revolver. The sea of miserable faces focused in her direction goaded her forward, fortifying her determination to stay strong. She picked her way across the soggy ground to collect the personal effects presented with honor.

The eleven baby steps seemed like a marathon but, though her legs wobbled, they held. Lacey pivoted, then appraised the two men whose suffering mirrored her own. The support and worry in their glassy eyes, offset by the twin lines of their clenched jaws, spurred her to make the return journey to their sides without delay.

When the ceremony concluded, strangers pressed against her on all sides as they encroached on the open grave. They either wanted to offer their genuine sympathy or to gawk at the morbid spectacle, maybe both. Misery threatened to drown her. She couldn't bear to witness Rob's sweet girlfriend, Gina, weep through another silk handkerchief or observe the droves of people he'd touched say goodbye. Even the open arms of Tyler's mom couldn't entice her to linger. Instead, she snagged a flower out of the elaborate spray at her feet, clutched it to her heart beneath Mason's coat, then turned to her brother's best friends.

"Get me out of here." The plea had barely crossed her lips before Ty sheltered her under his massive arm and Mason took point, clearing a path.

While he navigated a course around the headstones, she focused on tactical things. Things like how many place settings they'd need, the logistics of heating up the food generous neighbors and strangers alike had donated for Rob's farewell party, and the ripple of Tyler's six-pack against her ribs as he ushered her to Mason's waiting truck.

Only when they sandwiched her between them on the bench seat, isolating her from the morose gathering, did she surrender a tiny sigh. Mason turned over the big block engine with jerky motions of his stiff limbs as Tyler enfolded her hand in his, chafing it to infuse some semblance of warmth into the frigid digits.

"Take me home, please."

ABOUT THE AUTHOR

Jayne Rylon is a New York Times and USA Today bestselling author. She received the 2011 Romantic Times Reviewers' Choice Award for Best Indie Erotic Romance. Her stories used to begin as daydreams in seemingly endless business meetings, but now she is a full time author, who employs the skills she learned from her straight-laced corporate existence in the business of writing. She lives in Ohio with two cats and her husband, the infamous Mr. Rylon. When she can escape her purple office, she loves to travel the world, avoid speeding tickets in her beloved Sky, and–of course–read.

Jayne loves to chat with fans. You can find her at the following places when she's procrastinating:

Twitter: @JayneRylon
Facebook: http://www.facebook.com/jayne.rylon
Website: www.jaynerylon.com
Newsletter: www.jaynerylon.com/newsletter
Email: contact@jaynerylon.com

Made in the USA
Middletown, DE
25 October 2023